GOODBYE TSUGUMI

Banana Yoshimoto was born in 1964  the author of *Kitchen*, *N.P.*, *Lizard*, *Amrita* and *Asleep* ries, novels and essays have won numerous prizes b pan and abroad. She lives in Tokyo.

BANANA YOSHIMOTO

Goodbye Tsugumi

Translated from the Japanese by
Michael Emmerich

faber and faber

First published in the USA in 2002
by Grove Press, New York
First published in Great Britain in 2002
by Faber and Faber Limited
3 Queen Square London WC1N 3AU

Printed in England by Clays Ltd, St Ives plc

© Banana Yoshimoto, 1989
Translation © Michael Emmerich, 2002

Originally published in Japanese as Tsugumi by Chukoron Shinsha, Tokyo.
English translation rights arranged through Writers House LLC / Japan
Foreign Rights Centre.

The right of Michael Emmerich to be identified as translator
of this work has been asserted in accordance with Section 77 of the Copyright,
Designs and Patents Act 1988

A CIP record for this book
is available from the British Library

ISBN 0-571-21274-3

2 4 6 8 10 9 7 5 3 1

GOODBYE TSUGUMI

The Haunted Mailbox

It's true: Tsugumi really was an unpleasant young woman.

Leaving behind the town of my childhood, the quiet cycles of fishery and tourism that keep it running, I came to study at a certain university here in Tokyo. Now I'm having loads of fun, living in the city.

My name is Maria Shirakawa. I was named after the Virgin Mother.

Not that I'm particularly like her or anything—I'm not. And yet for some reason, all the new friends I've made since I moved to Tokyo tend to describe the way I am with words like "generous" and "levelheaded."

The truth is that I'm just a regular flesh-and-blood human being, and as a matter of fact I have a fairly short temper. Though in Tokyo I often catch myself wondering just what that's supposed to mean. People here are always getting angry about the smallest things—because it's raining, for instance, or because some class has been canceled, or because their dog took a leak in the wrong place. I guess maybe there is something slightly different about me. Because when I lose my temper, it only takes a moment before I feel the anger start to sweep back like a wave and sink down into the sand . . . For a long time I'd just assumed that this was because I grew up in the country, that I was just laid-back in the way country people are, but a few days ago this nasty professor refused to accept an essay of mine simply because I'd turned it in one minute late, and as I was walking back home, shaking with rage, glaring at the sunset, it suddenly occurred to me that there was another reason.

It's Tsugumi's fault—or rather, it's thanks to Tsugumi.

Everyone gets annoyed about something at least once a day, me included. But I noticed that there was something I did whenever this happened to me—that there was a sentence I would start chanting over and over deep down inside, like a sort of Buddhist chant, without even realizing that I was doing it. *Compared to the pain Tsugumi gives me, this is nothing at all.* It seemed that during the years I'd spent with Tsugumi, my body had come to understand in a hazy sort of way that, in the end, getting worked up really doesn't take you anywhere. And there was something else that I understood as I stared into the orange light of the gradually darkening sky—something that made me feel sort of like I wanted to cry.

For some reason it had occurred to me that love doesn't ever have to stop. *It's like the national water system,* I thought. *No matter how long you leave the faucets running, you can be sure the supply won't give out.*

This story you're reading contains my memories of the final visit I made to the seaside town where I passed my childhood—of my last summer at home. The various people from the Yamamoto Inn who appear as characters have now moved away, and it's unlikely that I'll ever have another opportunity to live with them. And so the only place left in this world to which my heart can return is there in the days I spent with Tsugumi, only there.

From the time she was born, Tsugumi was ridiculously frail, and she had a whole slew of physical ailments and defects. Her doctors announced that she would die young, and her family began preparing for the worst. Of course everyone around her spoiled her like you wouldn't believe. Her mother carted her around to hospitals all across Japan, not sparing any effort, offering up every ounce of her strength to try to extend Tsugumi's life even just a little. And so as Tsugumi toddled her unsteady way toward adulthood, she developed a personality that was just as pushy and insolent as it could be. She was strong enough that she could manage to lead a more or less normal life, but that just made matters worse. She was malicious, she was rude, she had a foul mouth, she was selfish, she was horribly spoiled, and to top it all off she was brilliantly sneaky. The obnoxious smirk that always appeared on her face after she'd said the one thing that everyone present definitely didn't want to hear—and said it at the most exquisitely wrong time, using the most unmistakably clear language and speaking in the ugliest, most disagreeable tone—made her seem exactly like the devil.

My mother and I lived in the guest house of the Yamamoto Inn. The inn was Tsugumi's house.

My father was in Tokyo, having an awful time trying to work out a divorce with the woman he was married to then. The two of them had already been living apart for ages, and he and my mother wanted to be officially married. This meant a lot of coming and going for him, and you would have thought it would be kind of grueling, but he and my mother were always daydreaming about the day when all three of us would be able to live together in Tokyo as a real family, without needing to keep a low profile. Having that dream to hold on to seemed to make their lives fairly enjoyable. So in the end, although the situation may have looked somewhat complicated from the outside, I grew up as the untroubled only child of a man and woman very deeply in love.

My mother's younger sister, Aunt Masako, had married into the Yamamoto family, and now my mother spent her days helping out in the kitchen of the Yamamoto Inn. The Yamamoto family was composed of the following four members: Uncle Tadashi, who managed the inn; Aunt Masako; and their two daughters, Tsugumi and her older sister, Yōko.

If I had to make a list of the Top Three Victims of Tsugumi's Outrageously Nasty Disposition, the order would undoubtedly be: Aunt Masako, then Yōko, then me. Uncle Tadashi kept his distance. I have to confess, though, that just putting myself on this list seems like kind of a bad joke, it's so presumptuous. In the process of raising Tsugumi, the top two contenders for the prize became so thoroughly gentle and good that they seemed almost to have entered the realm of angels.

While I'm at it, I might as well clarify the age relationships. Yōko is one year older than me, and I'm one year older than Tsugumi. Not that I've ever, ever been aware that Tsugumi is younger than me. You get the feeling that she's been the same ever since she was a little girl, that she's just continued growing into her badness.

Whenever her condition worsened and she was forced to take to her bed, Tsugumi's ferocious temper would acquire an even sharper, more awesome edge. In order to facilitate her convalescence, she'd been given a beautiful room on the third floor of the inn, a room originally meant for two. She had the best view in the whole building, one looking out over the ocean. During the day, sunlight glinted on the water, and whenever it rained the waves would turn rough and misty, and at night the lights of several squid boats could always be seen shining through the dark. The ocean out there was beautiful.

Being healthy, I can't even begin to imagine how frustrating it must be to live through day after day of ambiguity, more or less sure that you're going to die before long, but never entirely certain. There is one thing I *can* imagine, though, and that's that if I were spending as much time lying in that room as she did, I would want to make that seascape and the scent of the tide something irreplaceable, something central to my life. But evidently that wasn't how Tsugumi saw matters at all. She would do things like shred her curtains or keep the storm windows closed as tight as possible, and sometimes she'd turn over her dishes at meals, and then maybe throw all the books on her shelves across the tatami-matted floor, leaving her room in a state that reminded you of *The Exorcist* and making even her always-gentle family moan. At one point she got seriously into witchcraft, and started keeping dozens of "familiars" in her room—slugs and frogs and crabs and so on. (There were always plenty of crabs around, so they were particularly convenient.) Tsugumi began sneaking these critters into guests' bedrooms, and of course this led to complaints, so ultimately Aunt Masako and Yōko and even Uncle Tadashi were driven to tears, anguished at the way she was behaving.

But even at times like that, Tsugumi sneered. "You jerks sure are gonna feel like crap if I die tonight! Stop crying already!"

The smirk she wore looked oddly like the savior Maitreya's smile.

And it's true, Tsugumi was beautiful.

Long black hair, translucent white skin, and large, very large eyes. Eyelids with thick lines of long eyelashes that cast pale shadows whenever she let her gaze fall. Her arms and legs were long and slim, her veins seemed to lie just beneath the surface of her skin, and her body was small and tight—her physical appearance was so trim and gorgeous you could almost believe she was a doll fashioned that way by some god.

Ever since junior high, Tsugumi had made a sport of flirting with the boys in her class, getting them to come out with her for walks on the beach. Her boyfriends changed so often it was a joke, and you always had the feeling that in a town as small as ours she was bound to end up becoming the subject of some rather nasty rumors. But instead people just came to believe that her kindness and beauty totally overwhelmed everyone she came in contact with, leaving them hopelessly entranced. That's what the world saw of her—a façade so charming the real Tsugumi would have seemed like someone else entirely. I suppose in the end we should just be glad that she didn't make passes at the guests who came to stay at the inn. I bet she could have turned the place into a whorehouse if she'd wanted.

In the evening, Tsugumi and whichever boy she was messing around with at the time would walk out along the tall concrete embankment that lined the beach, where they could look out over the gradually dimming bay. Birds would be swirling low under the tinted sky as the glittering sighs of the waves rushed quietly toward them. The beach, empty except for a single dog that was still out running around, seemed to stretch on like a desert, wide and white, and out in the water there were a few boats being tossed about by the wind. Off in the distance, silhouettes of islands began fading into mist, and a line of clouds faintly gleaming with red was slipping away beyond the sea.

Tsugumi walks slowly, ever so slowly.

Worried, the boy offers her his hand. She takes it in her own thin hand, keeping her head turned to the ground. Then she lifts her face and gives him a little smile. Her cheeks shine in the light of the sinking sun, and her face seems achingly fragile, like the overwhelming brilliance of the twilight sky, which keeps changing from instant to instant, never lingering for long. Her white teeth, her thin neck, her large eyes as they gaze into his—it all gets mixed up with the sand and the wind and the sound of the waves, and seems on the verge of dropping away into nothing. And of course it's actually true: She could cease to exist at any moment and no one would be at all surprised.

Tsugumi's white skirt flaps back and forth in the wind.

Every time I witnessed one of these scenes, I'd mutter to myself that it was certainly convenient the way she could go around transforming herself into completely different people like that—and yet even as I was cursing her I'd find myself on the edge of tears. Even for me, who ought to have known her true character well enough, those scenes on the beach had an aura of sadness about them that struck chords somewhere deep within me, filling my chest with pain.

*   *   *

Tsugumi and I became very close friends as the result of a certain incident. Of course, we had known each other even as children. If you could manage to put up with her maliciousness and her vicious tongue, she was actually lots of fun to play with. As she imagined it, our little fishing town was a world without boundaries. Each grain of sand was a particle of mystery. She was smart and she liked to study, so her grades tended to be fairly high for someone who stayed home sick as often as she did, and then she was always reading books about all kinds of things, so she knew a lot. And of course one has to be fairly intelligent to start with, to think up so many different ways of being mean.

During the early years of elementary school, Tsugumi and I played a game called "The Haunted Mailbox." Our school was located at the base of a small mountain, and there was a garden out back. In the garden there was this old box that used to have a thermometer and a barometer and so on inside—classes had used it to study the weather—but now it was empty. The idea was that this box was connected to the spirit world and that letters from the other side would appear inside it. During the daytime we would go and put spooky stories or scary pictures that we had cut out of magazines inside, and then in the middle of the night we'd go back together and take them out. The garden where the box stood was an ordinary sort of place when the sun was up, but it certainly was frightening when you snuck out in the dark, and for a while we would both be totally absorbed in our game. But as time passed, "The Haunted Mailbox" got mixed up in all the other games we played back then, and eventually we forgot about it. In junior high I joined the basketball team, and practice was so demanding that I no longer had time to spend with Tsugumi. I'd fall asleep as soon as I got home, and there was always homework to do, and what with this and that she came to be nothing more than a cousin who lived next door. And then the incident occurred. As I recall, it was when I was in eighth grade, during spring vacation.

A light rain was falling that night, and I had been cooped up in my room. In seaside towns like ours the rain carries the scent of the tide. All around me was the rushing of raindrops plunging through the dark. I felt depressed from the very bottom of my heart. My grandfather had just died. I had lived in my grandparents' house until I was five, so I'd been really close to him. Even after my mother and I moved into the Yamamotos' guest house, and even now that I had entered junior high school, I had kept going to visit him, and we frequently exchanged letters. I'd stayed home from basketball practice that day, but I couldn't make myself do anything—I was just sitting there on the floor, slumped back against my bed, my eyes puffy from crying. At some point my mother came to the door of my room and called in to say that Tsugumi was on the phone, but I told her to say that I wasn't home. I didn't have the energy it took to be with Tsugumi. My mother knew as well as the rest of us how outrageous my cousin could be, so she just said that I was probably right, and walked off. I plopped back down on the floor and began flipping blankly through some magazine, and eventually began to nod off. And then I heard the sound of slippers padding toward my room from the opposite end of the hall. At the precise moment that I jerked up my head, the door slid smoothly open and I saw Tsugumi standing there, soaking wet.

She was panting. Clear drops of water kept dripping down

from the hood of her raincoat onto the tatami. Her eyes were wide open.

"Maria," she said, her voice feeble.

"Huh?" Still halfway caught in my dreams, I turned to look up at Tsugumi. She had an expression on her face like she was feeling uneasy, as if something had frightened her. When she spoke, however, her voice was bossy and urgent.

"Hey, would you wake up?! This is serious, kid! Look at this!"

Handling it extremely gently, as if it were something precious, she slipped a single sheet of paper from the pocket of her raincoat and held it straight out. I reached out vaguely with one hand, wondering why on earth she was acting in such an exaggerated way, and took the paper from her. The moment I saw what it was, I felt as if I'd suddenly been shoved under a spotlight, right in the dead center of the beam.

There was no doubt about it: The vigorous, semicursive characters written there were in my grandfather's hand. Handwriting that called up a soft ache of memories. The letter began as all his letters to me did:

Maria, my treasure,

Goodbye.
Take care of your grandmother, your father, and your mother. I hope you'll grow up to be a fine woman, worthy of the Virgin's name.

Ryūzō

I was shocked. For a moment an image of my grandfather floated through my mind—I saw his straight back as he sat facing his desk—and my chest felt as if it would burst. When I spoke, it was with incredible force.

"What is this? Where did you find it!"

Tsugumi looked straight into my eyes, her brilliant red lips trembling, and answered me in a touchingly earnest tone, as if she were saying a prayer.

"Can you believe it? In the haunted mailbox!"

"What? Are you serious!"

I had completely forgotten that old weather box, but now in a flash all the vanished memories returned. Tsugumi lowered her voice to a whisper.

"Listen, kid, I'm a hell of a lot closer to death than the rest of you assholes, so I can feel these things. I was in bed earlier, right, and the old guy showed up in my dream. Even after I woke up things felt kind of weird, you know? Sort of like there was something he had wanted to say. When I was a kid he used to buy all sorts of stuff for me too, so you might say I'm kind of indebted to him. The thing is, kiddo, that you were there in the dream too, and the old guy kind of seemed like he wanted to talk with you—after all he loved you most of all, right? So then it hit me. I went and took a peek in the mailbox, right, and damned if . . . Hey kid, did you ever tell him about the haunted mailbox while he was alive?"

"No," I shook my head. "I don't think so."

"Oh my God! Then this really is scary!" shouted Tsugumi, and then, her tone solemn, "Well, Maria, that damn box really was haunted, after all."

Now, pressing the palms of her hands together tightly and holding them before her chest, she closed her eyes. She seemed to be remembering herself running through the rain to the mailbox, just a short while ago. Even now the quiet sigh of the rainfall was echoing through the dark. I sensed reality slipping away from me as I was sucked deep into Tsugumi's night. Everything that had happened up to then, death and life, it all seemed to be sliding down into a whirlpool of mystery, a place where a different kind of truth held sway—that was the feeling, the softly uneasy stillness in the room.

"Maria, what on earth should we do?" Tsugumi said, her voice very quiet, and it sounded as if it had been a struggle for her to say even this much. Her face was terribly pale. She looked at me imploringly.

"Well, to begin with—" I said firmly. Just then Tsugumi had this peculiar air of delicacy about her, as if the immensity of what had happened was simply too much for her. "Don't say a word about this to anyone. But the most important thing of all is for you to go home right away, get yourself warmed up, and go to bed. It may be spring, but it's still raining outside—I'm sure you'll have a fever tomorrow. Hurry and change into some dry clothes. We can talk all this over in a day or two."

"Okay, I'll go then." Tsugumi wafted to her feet. "Later, babe."

Just before she left my room I said, "Tsugumi, thank you."

"Don't mention it, kid," Tsugumi replied.

And without a glance back, leaving the door open, she was gone.

For some time I sat there on the floor, rereading the letter again and again. Tears dripped down onto the carpet. A sweet, sacred warmth filled my chest. I felt the way I used to feel on Christmas morning when I woke to the sound of my grandfather's voice—*Well look here, there seems to be a present from Santa Claus!*—

and turned to see the wrapped gift lying by my pillow. The longer I kept reading, the less likely it seemed that my tears would ever stop. I slumped down over the letter and cried and cried and cried.

Okay, so maybe I was a little gullible.

I had my doubts, though! We're talking about Tsugumi, after all.

But those beautiful characters. The handwriting. The greeting that only my grandfather and I knew: "my treasure." Tsugumi soaked by the rain, and the power in her gaze, the way it had spiraled into me, and her tone of voice. And what's more, she had said with a totally serious face things she usually only said as a joke. *Listen, kid, I'm a hell of a lot closer to death than the rest of you assholes . . .* Oh yes, I had been magnificently deceived.

The punch line came the next day.

I went over to her house at noon, eager to have her tell me in more detail about the letter, but she wasn't home. I'd gone up to her room and was there waiting when Tsugumi's older sister, Yōko, came up to give me a cup of tea.

"I'm afraid Tsugumi's at the hospital," she said, somewhat sadly.

Yōko is short and round. She always speaks very mildly, almost as if she's singing. No matter what Tsugumi does to her, she remains soft and calm—the only thing that changes is that she gets this sad look on her face. It takes something almost unheard of to get her angry. She's the kind of person who really makes me feel small, you know, just being around her. Tsugumi went around jeering at Yōko, saying that she'd never met such a blockhead in her life and that the world would be a better place if she went and jumped in a lake, but I liked her a lot, and even looked up to her. There's no way anyone could live with Tsugumi and not find her trying, and yet whenever you saw Yōko she was smiling brightly. To me she really seemed like an angel.

"Is she feeling worse today?" I asked, worried.

I figured that going out in the rain had made her sick after all.

"Oh, not really . . . Lately she's been working herself much too hard, and so now she's started running a fever. I don't know exactly what she's doing, she seems to be writing some sort of letter or somethi—"

"She's what!" I shouted.

And then, as Yōko looked on in amazement, I turned around and ran my eyes over the shelves above her desk. Sure enough, there it was: *A Semicursive Calligraphy Workbook.*

She also had plenty of paper and ink, an inkstone, a very fine brush, and to top the whole thing off, a letter of my grandfather's that she had evidently stolen from my room.

Angry as I was, I was even more astounded.

What was it that made her carry these things so far? For someone like her who had never even held a brush properly, to produce calligraphy as skillfully executed as that in the letter would take an incredible amount of tenacity—I really couldn't imagine where it came from, or what purpose it served. The room was awash in spring sunlight. Dazed, I turned toward the window and looked out over the faintly glimmering ocean, allowing my thoughts to drift. Yōko was just opening her mouth to ask what had happened when Tsugumi returned.

Her face was flushed with fever, and she was leaning against Aunt Masako, taking small, listless steps, but the second she entered the room and saw my expression she gave a smug little grin. "Cat out of the bag?" she asked.

I felt so outraged and humiliated that in a flash my face turned bright red. Springing to my feet, I shoved her with all the strength I had.

"Ma-Maria!" cried Yōko, surprised.

Tsugumi crashed into the paper-paneled door, causing it to collapse, then flipped over and collided brutally with the wall. My aunt started to speak.

"Maria darling, please, Tsugumi isn't——"

I shook my head, tears streaming from my eyes.

"Please, just don't talk to me right now!" I cried, glaring ferociously at Tsugumi. I was so furious that even Tsugumi couldn't find anything to say. No one had ever pushed her or been at all violent with her before.

"If you've got so much time on your hands that crappy stuff like this is all you can find to do," I said, slamming *A Semicursive Calligraphy Workbook* down on the tatami floor, "then just drop dead! I don't care if you die!"

Perhaps at that moment, Tsugumi realized that unless she did something right away I would never have anything to do with her again for all of eternity—and that's precisely what I was planning to do—because, as she lay there, still in the position she'd landed in, she looked straight into my eyes, her gaze very clear, and mumbled the words she had refused to say all her life, no matter what happened, however awful things got, even if you tortured her.

"Sorry, Maria."

Aunt Masako and Yōko were both stunned, and I was more shocked than either of them. All three of us held our breath, unable to speak. The idea that Tsugumi would actually apologize to someone . . . no, it was completely unthinkable! And so we simply froze there, bathed in a brilliant flood of sunlight. The only sound we could hear was the far-off noise of wind blowing through the town, which had by now firmly settled into afternoon.

"Pnph-pnph. Pnha-ha-haw!" Suddenly Tsugumi erupted into laughter, shattering the stillness. "But seriously, Maria! You're *so* freaking gullible!" she said, writhing with new bursts of laughter. "I mean, what in the world were you thinking? Try using a little common sense, for God's sake! How the hell is a dead guy gonna write you a letter? Talk about dumb with a capital *D*! Aha-ha-ha!"

For some time, Tsugumi just kept rolling around the floor, whooping and holding her stomach as if she'd been suppressing the laughter the whole time and just couldn't manage to keep it inside anymore.

Seeing her like that, I burst out laughing myself. "Well, I guess there's no point in being angry now," I said, my face reddening, and then smiled again. The two of us reproduced the conversation we'd had during the rainfall the previous night for Yōko and my aunt, and the two of them stared in disbelief as we were swept up in round after round of riotous guffaws.

For better or worse, that's how Tsugumi and I ended up becoming such close friends.

Spring and the Yamamoto Sisters

Early this spring my father and his first wife were officially divorced, and my father telephoned to tell my mother and me that we could come to Tokyo. I'd already taken the entrance exam for a university in Tokyo, so my mother and I had been waiting for two calls at once: my father's, and the one that would tell me whether or not I had passed the test. This meant that for a while we both became extraordinarily sensitive to the ringing of our phone. And of course it was precisely at times like this that Tsugumi would abandon her usual policy and ring me up several times every day "just to say hello" or to ask if I'd "had bad news re the exam"— calls she knew would only grate on my nerves. For once, though, my mother and I were feeling so delighted with how things were going that we were able to respond perfectly cheerfully every time. "Oh, is that you, Tsugumi?" one or the other of us would say mildly, and as soon as we had said goodbye we'd forget that she had even called.

These were thrilling days. The joy of knowing that we were finally headed for Tokyo filled us with a bubbly, brilliant sense of anticipation. This was the period in our lives, in other words, when the winter snows began to melt.

My mother enjoyed working at the inn, but after all she had been there for ages and ages, and even when she was having a good time she was still waiting. Looking at her, you wouldn't have thought she was suffering much, but that was only because by acting as though she were having fun she managed to keep her suffering down to a minimum. I suspect this blithe surface of good humor is also what gave my father the heart he needed to go on commuting back and forth so diligently, instead of just giving my mother up. Not that she's such a strong person—she really isn't— but you got the feeling that part of her was struggling to become strong, even if she herself didn't know it. Every so often I'd over- hear her complaining to Aunt Masako, but she always spoke so cheerfully that the complaints didn't sound as grave as the prob- lems would lead you to expect, and I had the sense that even as Aunt Masako kept laughing and nodding, she was having trouble deciding how she ought to respond. And of course when you get down to brass tacks—well, no matter how kindly people treated my mother, she was still leeching off her sister's family, still liv- ing as my father's mistress, and there was no sign that things would ever improve. Even if she kept all this locked up inside, I'm sure there were plenty of times when the uncertainty of it all left her feeling so worn out that she just wanted to break down and cry. And since I thought I could understand some of what she was going through, I ended up becoming an adult without ever having passed through a rebellious stage, the way most adolescents do.

Come to think of it, that seaside town where my mother and I lived for so many years, waiting for my father—it's shown me all kinds of things.

Now that spring was drawing near, and each day was warmer than the last, and now that we were finally going to leave, all the everyday, nothing-special scenes I was so used to seeing, like the aging corridors of the inn, and all those swarms of bugs that gathered in the light of the sign out front, and the poles where we hung laundry, where spiders liked to spin their webs and beyond which the mountains jutted up . . . suddenly all of these hit me harder, with greater clarity. The inn seemed bathed in a haze of light.

Toward the end, I started going for walks along the beach every morning, taking along an Akita dog with the rather uninspired name of Pooch. Pooch belonged to the Tanakas, who lived in the house just behind the inn.

Early mornings when the sky was clear the ocean always seemed to shine with a special brilliance. Something about the way the hundreds of millions of shimmering waves kept blinking into disarray and then rising up to start rolling forward again, with that chilly look to them—something in it seemed sacred, made you feel as if you had to keep your distance. Pooch would dash out and frisk around on the beach, running wherever he wanted to, stopping here and there to enjoy the affections of people out fishing, while I sat at the edge of the concrete embankment, looking out over the water.

I can't remember exactly when it happened, but somewhere along the way Tsugumi started joining us on our walks. This made me really happy.

Once, back when Pooch was still just a puppy, Tsugumi had bullied him so long and so relentlessly that he'd finally gotten desperate and given her hand the nastiest bite he could manage. Yōko and Aunt Masako and my mother and I were just sitting down to lunch when it happened. I can still picture the scene: Aunt Masako said, "I wonder where Tsugumi is?" and the very next moment Tsugumi stepped into the room with her hand streaming blood and her face just as pale as it could be. "Tsugumi, what happened!" shouted my aunt, leaping up from where she sat on the floor. And Tsugumi replied coolly, "The worm has turned." The tone in which she said this was so hilarious that Yōko and my mother and I all exploded into laughter. But ever since that day, Pooch and Tsugumi had hated each other's guts, and whenever Tsugumi went out the back door Pooch always started barking so wildly that we all got really worried, thinking that it might annoy the guests. Since I got along with both of them, their mutual animosity had always troubled me in a vague sort of way, and now that I was going to be moving away it was especially nice to see that they had patched up their differences.

Tsugumi came out with us as long as it wasn't raining. I would slide my window open in the morning, and as soon as Pooch's ears caught that sound he would come flying out of his doghouse, practically jiggling with excitement. I would hurry and wash my face and change into my clothes, then go outside and quietly push open the gate that separated the rear of the Yamamoto Inn from the Tanakas' back garden. Pooch would be frolicking around, jangling his heavy chain, I'd catch hold of him and buckle on his leather leash, and then we'd walk back out through the gate. It was never really clear to me exactly when Tsugumi came out, but she was always there, waiting for us. At first, having her around put Pooch in kind of a grumpy mood, and even though Tsugumi tried not to let it show, you could tell that she was feeling a bit antsy herself, and wasn't at all sure how to behave. So in the beginning our walks together tended to have sort of a gloomy atmosphere to them. Then Pooch warmed up to Tsugumi, and finally even started letting her hold his leash. I'd watch her being jerked along in the morning sunlight, shouting, "Slow down, you dumb mutt!" but obviously having a terrific time, and I'd realize just how adorable she could be. *Deep down Tsugumi really wanted to be friends with Pooch, after all!* I thought, feeling a quiet surge of tenderness. Of course if Pooch started running on ahead too quickly or anything like that Tsugumi would give his leash such a brutal jerk that he'd end up standing on his hind legs, so I couldn't take my eyes off her for a second. It definitely would not have been good to have her vaporize the neighbor's dog.

The amount of exercise we got on our walks seemed to be just right for Tsugumi. Since she'd started coming with us, I'd cut the length of the walk in half. I'd been worried that it still might be too far, but her complexion improved and she didn't run a fever, so I decided it was probably okay.

I remember the walk we took one morning.

It was a gorgeous day, without a single cloud in the sky, and the color of the ocean and the sky struck you as being vaguely sweet—they were that shade of blue. Everything glinted with gold in the morning sun, so bright you could hardly stand to keep your eyes open, and the outlines of things were pale and fuzzy the way they are sometimes in movies. About halfway down the beach there was a tall wooden platform shaped like a castle turret. During the summer months lifeguards stood up there and kept an eye on the swimmers. Tsugumi and I climbed the ladder to the platform. Pooch kept circling around the base for a while, looking up enviously at us, but when he realized there was no way he could climb up after us he gave up and trotted off down the beach, pretty far away. Tsugumi shouted, "Serves you right, jerk!" in an unbelievably spiteful tone, and Pooch answered with a woof.

"What makes you say things like that?" I asked, astonished.

"Hell, that damn dog even understands Japanese!" Tsugumi said, grinning. She had her face turned to the ocean, and her thin bangs kept swishing across her forehead, all the tiny hairs lightly jostling together. She had run a really incredible distance, and now her cheeks were bright red and you could see the veins under her skin. Her glittering eyes reflected the water.

I looked at the ocean, too.

It's a marvelous thing, the ocean. For some reason when two people sit together looking out at it, they stop caring whether they talk or stay silent. You never get tired of watching it. And no matter how rough the waves get, you're never bothered by the noise the water makes or by the commotion of the surface— it never seems too loud, or too wild.

I simply couldn't believe that I was about to move to a place where there was no ocean. Somehow it didn't register; it was so strange that just thinking about it made me uneasy. Because the ocean had always been there, in the good times as well as the bad times of my life, when it was sweltering out and the beach was filled with people, and in the dead of winter when the sky was heavy with stars, and when we were heading to the local shrine on New Year's Day . . . all I had to do was turn my head and it would be there, the same as always. It didn't matter if I was a kid or a grown-up. The old woman next door might have just died, the local doctor might have just had a baby, or I might be on my first date or have fallen out of love—none of this made any difference at all to the ocean; it remained just as it was, fanning out around the edge of our town and zooming quietly off into the distance, the tide rising and falling just as it always did, no matter what. On days when the visibility was particularly good you could easily make out the shore on the far side of the bay. And it seemed to me that even if you weren't actively letting your emotions ride its surface, the ocean still went on giving you something, teaching you some sort of lesson. Perhaps that was why I had never actually considered its existence before—never really thought about the thundering of the waves as they sweep in endlessly toward the shore. But since I was thinking about it, what on earth did people in the city turn to when they felt the need to reckon with "balance"? Maybe the moon? That seemed like the obvious choice. But then the moon was so small and far away, and something about it felt sort of lonely, and it didn't seem like it would really help . . .

"Tsugumi, I don't think I can live without the ocean nearby," I blurted out suddenly, without thinking. "I'm too used to having it here."

Now that I had actually put the feeling into words, I began to realize with increasing clarity how nervous I really was. With every moment that passed, the early sun grew whiter and stronger. Off in the distance we could hear the innumerable sounds that spread through the town as it woke.

"God, you're a moron!" Tsugumi snapped. She sounded furious, and she kept her face turned toward the water. "Whenever you get something in this world, you lose something too—that's just the way things work. The three of you are finally going to be living together, right? Mom, Dad, and baby Maria, one happy little family! You've succeeded in chasing off the old wife, haven't you? What more could you want? What's

23

an ocean compared to all that, Maria? You're such a freaking child, you know that?"

"Yeah . . . I guess you're right," I said, struggling to hide my confusion.

Tsugumi's response had been so honest and to the point that it left me shaken. So much so that for a moment the unease I'd felt was completely blown away. Could I understand this to mean that somewhere deep down inside Tsugumi was also "getting" and "losing" things, and just kept those feelings to herself? She'd always seemed so comfortable with herself, so independent and strong that you could never have imagined her getting and losing things that way . . . All of a sudden I felt as if she had come into focus for me, and for the first time I could see her clearly— a strange, overwhelming sadness.

Has she just kept all this hidden from us?

Is that really how she feels?

Time passed as I continued doing the things that needed to be done before I could leave the town of my childhood. One by one, I tried to come to terms with all the things I would miss. I got together briefly with some friends from junior high whom I hadn't seen in ages and saw the guy I'd gone out with in high school, and told them that I would be moving away. I had the feeling that this need to do everything so properly was something I'd inherited from my mother, and somehow this touched me deeply. Maybe it had something to do with the position she had been in as my father's mistress, I don't know, but she had always taken great care when she interacted with people to treat them very politely, very properly. To tell the truth,

I'd actually intended to make a more stylish exit when the time came, sashaying away without saying a word to anyone. But my mother made such a display of going around to all the neighbors to say her goodbyes, and she acted so genuinely sorry to be leaving that I could see everyone in our small town would end up hearing the news before very long. Of course this meant I would have to switch my own tack. In the end I made up my mind just to go ahead and get together with anyone I felt like seeing.

Also, little by little, I started to pack up the things in my room.

Packing was a task that put me in a luminously beautiful, heartrending frame of mind. A mood that recalled the waves. It didn't matter where I was in the job, suddenly I would just stop in the middle of what I was doing and stay perfectly still, and once again the knowledge that this work was leading me to an inescapable, but certainly not unhappy, parting—a natural separation—would gush into me. And every time this happened I would realize that this feeling wasn't quite suffering, no, but a kind of distress that was at the same time wonderfully exciting. Even as I rested there this sea of emotions continued to ebb and flow through my chest.

Tsugumi's sister Yōko and I had part-time jobs working at the same shop, a bakery on the main street in town, well known in the area for being the only place around that dealt exclusively in Western desserts. (I'm not sure that really gives them the right to brag, but hey . . .)

That night, I was supposed to pick up my last paycheck. I waited until just before the store closed, since that was the shift

Yōko was working, and just as I'd hoped, we each ended up going home with a box of leftover cakes.

Yōko had stacked the boxes very gently in the basket of her bike, which she was now pushing alongside her. I walked next to her, keeping my pace nice and slow. The gravel path that led to the Yamamoto Inn followed the bank of a river and eventually ran into this big bridge. The sea opened into view on the other side of the bridge, and the river flowed quietly into it. The light of the moon and the streetlamps shone brightly on the water and the railings of the bridge.

We had almost reached the bridge when Yōko cried out, "Wow, look at all the flowers!" Her gaze was directed down under the bridge. The bank around its base had been hardened with cement, but in the little patch of dirt that still remained, a clump of white flowers was in full bloom, swaying lightly back and forth in the night wind.

"God, there are so many!" I said.

The whiteness of the flowers seemed to levitate in the dark. Every time the crowd of petals bobbed under a puff of wind you were left with an afterimage of white that had the texture of a dream. And just beside that dream the river continued to flow, and off in the distance the dark nighttime ocean stretched the glow of the moon into a single gleaming road. The black waters before us swelled up and fell back again, glimmering with tiny flecks of light, the dark motion extending all the way to infinity.

I won't have the luxury of seeing scenes like this much longer, I thought, letting the sadness bloom gently in my mind. I didn't say anything to Yōko. She had been crying a lot lately, and I didn't want to make her lonely.

26

We stopped and stood still for a moment.

"It's pretty, isn't it?" I said.

"Very." Yōko gave me a little smile.

Her long hair rippled lightly down her shoulders. Compared to Tsugumi, she wasn't the sort of person who really stood out for her great looks, but her face was elegantly proportioned. For some reason both she and Tsugumi had very fair skin, even though they had grown up so close to the ocean. Under the light of this moon, Yōko looked even paler than usual.

Soon we started walking on toward the house. In another ten minutes we would be eating the cakes that were now bumping around in the basket of the bicycle. The scene seemed to rise up before my eyes: the clamor of the television, the fragrance of the tatami; four women enjoying each other's company. Yōko and I would saunter into the brightly lit living room, where my mother and Aunt Masako would be sitting, and announce that we were back. Tsugumi would grumble that she was "sick to hell of eating all these freebie cakes you morons are always bringing home," but even so she would pick out three or four that she liked and retreat with them to her room. Because that's what she always did. As she put it, "I hate this home-is-where-the-heart-is garbage. It makes me want to puke."

We continued walking. Even when we had stepped into some scrunched-up side street where you couldn't see the ocean, the roar of the waves would follow us. Just as the moon followed us. There beyond and beyond the rows of old roofs, always— the moon.

As cheery and bright as we knew things would be when we arrived home, Yōko and I both felt vaguely dispirited as we ambled on. Maybe it was because, starting today, I no longer worked at the bakery. A loneliness heavy enough to balance out all the years the two of us had spent together as cousins and good friends echoed between us like the faint strains of a melody. Maybe I'd started thinking again about Yōko and what she was like, the translucent silhouette of a petal fluttering down to the ground against the glare of the sun—a petal from a flower named *gentleness*. No, no—in fact it wasn't like that at all. We were just walking along talking about silly things, giggling—that was it. And yet no matter how much fun I seemed to be having at the time, sometimes when I think back over my memories all that comes to mind is the blackness of the night and the shadows of telephone poles and garbage cans, things like that, very dark, and the images make me heartsick. When I remember that night now, it seems that's how it really was.

"You said you were going to come just before the store closed," said Yōko, "so I was betting that the manager would let us have the leftover cakes. I was looking forward to it the whole time. I'm so happy he did!"

"It's true. He doesn't always let us have them, and sometimes there aren't any left over anyway. We lucked out tonight," I replied.

Yōko smiled. "When we get home we can have a little party!"

Even in profile her face looked gentle. She had on her round glasses.

"Hey Yōko . . . I really, really want to have one of those apple pies before Tsugumi takes them all. You know how much she likes apple pie."

It's kind of pathetic, but I think my tone was pretty desperate at the time.

28

"Well there aren't any apple pies in this box, so we just have to make sure only to show her this one. How does that sound?" She smiled again.

Yōko is smart enough to accept all the little selfish demands that people make, no matter what it is they're asking. It was sort of like sand soaking up water. The environment she'd grown up in seemed to have given her a kind of cheerfully levelheaded way of looking at things.

Setting Tsugumi aside for the moment, since her personality is somewhat unique, I had a number of friends at school who were like Yōko, the daughters of families that ran inns. And no matter how different they all were as types, there was something they all shared. I'm only talking here about the general sort of aura they had—I want to stress that—but you really did get the sense that they had all mastered the art of keeping interpersonal relations nice and dry. I guess it's because, from the time they were children, people had always been coming to live in their houses for a while and then going off again, and they had all grown up seeing this, having it there all the time in the background. Perhaps you could say that they'd just been totally goodbyed out, and that they were great at masking the various emotions that get called up when the time comes to part with someone you know. I'm not actually the child of one of these families, but I'm pretty close to being one, and I have a feeling that I tend to deal with things in the same way. I think I'm good at running away from the pain that comes with these ordinary emotions.

But when it came to goodbyes, Yōko was different from the rest of us.

When we were kids we used to run around while the maids were cleaning the rooms and doing that sort of stuff, and every once in a while guests who were staying for long periods of time would come over and say hello and ask if we were the owners' children, and we'd get friendly with them. Even if we just knew them enough to recognize them, it was still fun to say hello when we met. And for every truly unpleasant guest there would be one who was really wonderful, who made everyone feel good just by being around. They were the kind of people whose presence seems to light up a gathering, who become popular with the cooks and the part-time staff and end up as one of the main topics of their conversation. And when the time came for these men and women to leave and they packed up their belongings and climbed into their cars and waved and then drove off, the afternoon light that spilled down into the hollow emptiness of their rooms always seemed so bright you could hardly stand to look. You knew they would probably come again next year, but next year seemed so distant and abstract. Then another guest would come and stay in the same room. It was a cycle we had all been through again and again and again. An inescapable part of our lives.

Toward the beginning of autumn, when the tourist season drew to a close and the number of guests rapidly declined, I'd always manage to muddle my way through the loneliness by forcing myself to be very boisterous and cheery. But Yōko wandered around looking as if she felt all alone in the world, and if she came across something that had been forgotten by one of the kids she'd been friendly with she would even start to cry. The part of people that feels this kind of loneliness is actually very small, and I think anyone who really tries can get by without suffering from it at all. All you have to do is keep the spotlight turned in some other direction. It's perfectly obvious that letting yourself focus on that area is what makes you get all sentimental and lonely, so the more opportunities you have to experience these goodbyes the more skilled you should become at distracting yourself, and thus at coping with these little lonelinesses. And yet Yōko had done precisely the opposite. Something in her had continued protecting that feeling, had nurtured that loneliness, taking special care to keep it safe. I suppose she didn't want to lose it.

As soon as you turned the corner you would see the sign of the Yamamoto Inn glowing out from among the bushes. Every time I saw that sign, and saw the long line of guest room windows, I would relax a little, feel a kind of relief. It didn't matter whether there were lots of guests and lights shining in most of the rooms, or whether the whole place was empty and the windows were dark; either way it felt like I was being welcomed back by something big, something much larger than me. We would go around to the kitchen side of the inn and slide open the door to the main house, and Yōko would call in, "We're back!" At that hour my mother was either still over in the inn or else sitting having a cup of green tea in the living room of the main house. Once we'd finished our cakes and pies and whatever else, my mother and I would head back over to the guest house. That was the routine. It had been like that for ages.

"You know what?" I said, as we were taking off our shoes, remembering something I'd been planning to do. "I've been thinking I'll just give you that album you asked me to tape for you. Why don't I go get it now?"

"Huh? Oh, but I couldn't take it from you! It's a two-record set, isn't it? Just a tape would be fine," Yōko said, looking stunned.

"No, really, I don't mind. I was planning to leave it behind anyway; you'll be doing me a favor if you take it." I realized as I was speaking that this wasn't a topic I should have brought up now, but my mouth simply wouldn't stop. "Think of it as my going-away present. Hold on, is that right? Can I call it a going-away present when I'm giving it to you?"

I glanced over at Yōko. She was in the shadowy part of the entryway, near the door, putting the cover over her bike. She had her face turned down and her cheeks and forehead were red. There were tears in her eyes.

These were such honest, heartfelt tears that I had no idea how to react, and so I pretended not to notice. I stepped up into the house. Without turning around, I called out, "Hurry on in. I'm ready for some cake!"

Yōko hurriedly wiped away her tears and nodded. "Okay, I'll be right in," she said, in a voice that made it clear her nose was clogged. She was lovely, wonderfully pure. I bet she thought no one knew how easily she cried.

For ten years I had been protected, wrapped up in something like a blanket that had been stitched together from all kinds of different things. But people never notice that warmth until after they've emerged. You don't even notice that you've been inside until it's too late for you ever to go back—that's how perfect the temperature of that blanket is. For me it was the ocean, the whole town, the Yamamoto family, my mother, and a father who lived far away. All this embraced me back then, ever so softly. Now I'm having lots of fun, and I'm really happy here in

Tokyo, but every once in a while the memory of my life in that town hits me so hard that I can hardly stand it, and I start feeling sad. At times like that the very first memories that are resurrected in my mind are these two scenes: Tsugumi playing with Pooch on the beach and Yōko smiling as she walks down the path that night, pushing her bicycle beside her.

Life

Now that the three of us were all living together, my father seemed to get such a kick out of coming home every evening that he hardly knew what to do with himself. He was so buoyant that just looking at him made you smile. Night after night he brought home sushi or cakes or some other little treat, and when he yanked open the door and called out, "I'm home! Hey, I'm home!" he would have such a soppy grin on his face and his expression would be so totally relaxed that I would start to feel slightly uneasy, wondering if he was really managing to focus on his work at the office. On Saturdays and Sundays he would insist on driving my mother and me around to all these nice stores and good restaurants he knew, carting us all over the city, or maybe he would cook up something for us himself, and then he'd become a carpenter for the day and put up a bunch of shelves over my desk that I'd told him again and again I didn't particularly need, and then . . . let me tell you, it got to be pretty crazy. He was The Dad Who Came Late. But it's true that his eagerness succeeded in skimming away the fine particles of unease that had continued to circulate among us. All the little knots that the years had put in our lives came undone, and we began to function as a proper family.

One evening my father called home from work and told us sadly that he was going to have to stay late that night. My mother popped off to bed pretty early, but I stayed up at the table in the combined dining room and kitchen, writing up an essay for school while watching TV, and I was still working there when my father came home. He smiled when he saw me, looking pleased.

"Still up?" he said. "I guess your mother has gone to bed?"

"Yeah," I replied. "Fish and miso soup is all there is, but if you want some dinner I can warm it up for you . . ."

"Sounds great."

My father dragged his chair back a little from the table and sat down, then took off his blazer. I set the pot of soup on the stove and put the plate of broiled fish into the microwave. All at once a wave of energy sparked into the kitchen, electrifying the night. The murmur of the TV kept flowing on quietly through the room.

Suddenly my father spoke. "Hey Maria, want a senbei?"

"Huh?" I said, looking back over my shoulder.

My father was just removing two rice crackers wrapped in paper from his briefcase, making a sort of bumbling, crumply paper noise but handling them extremely carefully. He put them down on the table.

"One is for your mother."

"I'm confused. Why do you have only two?" I asked, puzzled.

"Someone from another company came in today and he brought a box of these along as a little present," explained my father. "I had one and it was so delicious that, well, you know, I kind of snuck these out for the two of you. Trust me, these senbei are really, really good."

The man wasn't even blushing.

"God, Dad, didn't anyone catch on? You're like a little boy with a dog hidden behind the house or something," I said, laughing. I mean, picture a grown man waiting around until the coast is clear so that he can slip two senbei into his briefcase and take them home! Give me a break!

"The vegetables in Tokyo are awful, right, and the seafood is so gross you can hardly stand to eat it. But it turns out that the senbei here are great—it's the one food this city can really be proud of," said my father, speaking between mouthfuls of the rice and miso soup I had served him. I took his fish out of the microwave and set it down on the table in front of him.

"Well then, perhaps I'll indulge myself," I said, sitting down at the table and picking up one of the two packages. I felt the way non-Japanese must feel when they encounter senbei for the first time. With the very first bite I took, the intense flavor of the soy sauce in the coating flooded my mouth. It really was delicious. I told my father this, and he nodded contentedly.

I remember a time, soon after my mother and I came to Tokyo, when I caught sight of my father on his way home from work. I had just been to see a movie, and I was waiting for a traffic light at the corner of two streets lined with office buildings. The sky was brilliant with rays from the setting sun, and the subtle wash of its colors was reflected with infinite clarity in the rows of windows that covered the buildings, as vividly as if they were mirrors. It was right around the time when people get out of work, and a crowd of men dressed in suits and office ladies who had changed out of their uniforms into the livelier variety of their everyday clothes had gathered at the crosswalk, waiting for the light to change. The breeze that was blowing and the expressions on people's faces seemed slightly tired, tired in precisely the same way. The workers kept chatting back and forth, and they all had these really ambiguous smiles on their faces that made it hard to tell whether or not they had places to go from here. The faces of the few men and women who were standing silently on their own seemed slightly severe.

All of a sudden my attention shifted to this guy who was walking along on the other side of the street. For a moment it seemed kind of strange that he should draw my eye so much, but then I realized that there was a very good reason—the guy was my father. My dad was marching along with the same severe expression on his face as the people I'd just been looking at, which felt really strange. The only time he wore this kind of expression at home was when he was watching TV and he lay down to get more comfortable and then started nodding off: His faced always assumed an expression like that the instant before he finally zonked out. I gazed at my father's "public face," utterly fascinated. And then this office lady came running out of the building where my father worked, shouting his name. He stopped walking. From where I stood on the other side of the street I was able to see everything that happened. The woman had an envelope in her hands that looked like it must be full of papers. My father's eyes darted back and forth for a moment or two until he located her. Then he was smiling and moving his lips, probably saying something like *God, what an idiot I am! Sorry to put you to so much trouble!* and the woman hurried over to where he was standing, panting slightly, and handed him the envelope.

She gave him a little smile and bowed lightly, he said goodbye to her, and then she went back into the building and my father started walking on briskly toward the subway, holding the envelope in both hands. Just then the light changed and crowds of people spilled out into the street. I deliberated for a few moments about whether to chase after him or not, but decided that it was too late now, he was too far away, and gave up. I remained standing there a little while with the dusky city around me, letting my thoughts wander . . .

As brief as this episode was, and though it was just an ordinary instance of ordinary forgetfulness, it gave me an unintended glimpse of the life my father had been living before we joined him. A life he had lived for a very, very long time. For every single month and year that my mother and I had lived in that town near the sea my father had passed a month and a year here, breathing this city air—he had made his way through just as many days as we had. Arguing with his former wife, working at his job, making a name for himself, eating meals, forgetting things like he had just now, pausing every so often to think of my mother and me living in that town, so far away . . . And while for the two of us the town had been a home, the scene of our everyday lives, in my father's mind it was probably just a place you visited on the weekends, somewhere you went to relax. Perhaps there had even been times when he felt like giving up on us, just chucking my mother and me away and being done with the whole thing? *You know,* I thought, *I bet there were.* Of course he would probably never mention any of this to the two of us, but sometimes deep down inside he must have felt that the whole thing was more trouble than it was worth. We had been in such a bizarre situation that we ended up acting like characters in just the opposite scenario, as gentle and good as the members of some Typical Happy Family. Though we weren't aware of it, we were all struggling to conceal the murky snarl of emotions that must actually have slept deep inside each one of us. *Life is a performance,* I thought. Perhaps the word "illusion" would have meant more or less the same thing, but to me "performance" seemed closer to the truth. Standing there in the midst of the crowd that evening, I felt this realization swirl dizzily through my body in a dazzling splendor of light, if only for an instant. Each one of us continues to carry the heart of each self we've ever been, at every stage along the way, and a chaos of everything good and rotten. And we have to carry this weight all alone, through each day that we live. We try to be as nice as we can to the people we love, but we alone support the weight of ourselves.

"Dad, don't push yourself so much that you burn out, okay?" I said.

My father looked up at me, his face blank with surprise.

"What do you mean? Push myself at what?"

"You know, coming home early and buying little presents for us and going around buying me new clothes and things like that. If you do that stuff too much, eventually it's going to wear you down."

"What's that last example? I haven't bought you any clothes."

My father was grinning. I grinned back at him.

"No, but I'm still hoping," I said.

"What do you mean when you say that I'll burn out?"

"Oh, you know. All of a sudden you'll get bored with family life, and then you'll start an affair with someone or go around getting drunk all the time, or maybe just start taking your frustration out on us, that kind of thing."

"It's true, eventually something like that might even happen." Once again a smile drifted across his face. "But you know, right now I'm using every ounce of my energy to try to put together a new life with you and your mother. After all these years of waiting, we're finally living the way I've always wanted to, and let me tell you, I'm really having a ball. I know there are some men out there who enjoy living on their own, who actually do prefer that kind of life, but that's not the way I am. I've always been more of the comfy stay-at-home type. To tell the truth, that's the reason things didn't work out with my first wife. She didn't like children, but she loved to go out. Keeping house wasn't really her thing, either. Of course it's only natural that there are people like her, and there's no problem with that, but I wanted the sort of family where you all sit down and watch TV together every night and, even though it's a pain in the butt, the whole family goes out together on Sundays. You know what I mean, right? The sort of family where you all feel really close to one another. Ultimately it was just a mistake for the two of us to fall in love. And so now when I think back over all the years I had to live here apart from you and your mother, when I think about all the different shades of loneliness I got to know during those years, I can really understand how crucial friends and family and people like that are. Of course it's possible that I'll come to see things in a different light later on, and maybe I will end up doing some really hurtful things to the two of you, but when you get right down to it stuff like that is part of life too. Maybe one day our inner workings will get out of sync, it's true—but even if that's going to happen, precisely because that might happen, it's better for us to make lots of good memories for our-selves now, while we can."

My father had stopped eating while he talked. His tone of voice had a cool, matter-of-fact feel to it, and I found myself impressed that he'd managed to hit exactly the right note. This dad of mine sometimes says some pretty good stuff! A kind of tenderness spread slowly through my chest—a feeling that I hadn't yet experienced since we'd moved to Tokyo.

"I'm sure your mother has all kinds of things on her mind, too," said my father gently. "She doesn't talk about it, but after all it's only natural to hurt a bit when you've left a place where you lived for so long, right?"

"What makes you think she's hurting?"

"Take this, for instance." My father tapped the slice of mack-erel with his chopsticks. "Lately we've been having fish every night."

Once he'd pointed it out, I realized it was true. An image of my mother halting in her tracks when she came to the fish store drifted up into my mind, and I fell silent.

"Hey, I thought you were supposed to be a college student," said my father suddenly. "Don't you have any parties to go to or a job or anything like that? You always seem to be at home in the evenings."

"What are you talking about, Dad? It's not like there are that many parties for me to be going to in the first place—I'm not in any clubs or anything. And no, I don't have a job. What makes you come out with all this straight-from-TV-stereotype stuff all of a sudden?" I said, laughing.

"Oh, you know . . . at least once in my life I want to try out that 'concerned dad' thing: 'Listen here, you've been staying out a little bit too late recently, haven't you!' and all that." My father laughed with me.

The senbei for my mother remained on the table after everything else had been cleared away, an unobtrusive symbol of our family's happiness.

Still, every once in a while I would find myself gripped by a longing for the ocean so intense that I couldn't get to sleep. And no way to escape the feeling.

Sometimes when the wind changes in Ginza—a part of Tokyo I often walk around—all of a sudden you find yourself bobbing in the salty scent of the tide. During the few moments that the scent remains, I always feel as if I'm about to burst out screaming. This isn't a lie, and I'm not exaggerating. Suddenly my whole body is drawn into the swirl of this fragrance, and I ache so fiercely that I can't even make myself move. I feel like bursting into tears. Usually when this happens the weather is lovely, and the clear sky stretches on and on into the distance, and I feel like hurling away the bags I'm carrying from Yamano Records or Printemps or wherever, and dashing off to stand on that dirty concrete embankment beneath which the tide is forever dawdling, and just keep drinking in the aroma of the sea until my heart is full. It occurs to me that perhaps this is what people mean by "nostalgia": the pain of knowing that this powerful yearning will eventually fade.

This happened again just a few days ago when I was out walking with my mother. It was near noon on a weekday, and there weren't very many people out and about on the broad avenue. My mother and I had just emerged from a department store when a powerful gust of wind crashed down on top of us, bringing with it the scent of the ocean. We both recognized it immediately.

"What is that? It smells like salt water," said my mother.

"It must be from over that way, you know . . . from Harumi Wharf," I said, pointing in the general direction of the wharf. I felt like one of those people who like to lick their fingers and check which way the wind is blowing.

"I guess you're right," replied my mother. She gave me a little smile.

She had been saying she wanted to go buy some flowers from the florist by the entrance to the park, so we headed in that direction. Way off down the street we could see the leaves of the trees, looking as if they had soaked up tons of water, dazzlingly green. Their color stood out beautifully against the blue of the sky, which was itself very precious—weather this nice is rare in the rainy season. A bus drove by, headed, as it happened, toward Harumi Wharf. The rumble of its massive form lingered in my ear.

"Should we stop for some tea before we go home?" I asked.

"No, we'd better hurry back. I'm going to my ikebana class this afternoon, and you know how your father is. He's leaving tomorrow for that business trip, you know. If I don't get something ready ahead of time so we can all sit down and have dinner together, he'll get all mopey again. I swear, he's just like a child, isn't he? It's just crazy." I glanced at my mother's profile as she said this, and saw that she was smiling.

"It's only temporary," I said. "He'll settle down."

Since she'd stepped into her role as a wife, my mother's face had started to look more round, and that roundness stayed with her even when she smiled. As the corners of her mouth rose, the outline of her face seemed to send slow ripples circling out into the soft rays of sunlight that fell around her.

"So Maria, have you made some friends at school? I guess you must have, since people are always calling. But are you enjoying college?"

"Sure I'm enjoying it. Why?"

"Oh, you know. Before we came here you always had Yōko and Tsugumi to talk to, right? They were like sisters to you. So I thought maybe you would feel a little lonely in Tokyo. I mean, it's so quiet in our house here."

"Yeah," I said. "It's true, it is pretty quiet."

The busy sound of footsteps rushing back and forth in the halls of the inn. The commotion in the kitchen, the echoing moan of the big vacuum cleaner, the ringing of the phone in the lobby. There were always crowds of people in the house making all different noises, and at five and nine o'clock the Town Association would broadcast a message from the speakers that hung here and there around the town telling kids that it was time for them to head home. The thundering of waves, whistles of trains, the chirping of birds.

"I bet you're probably lonelier than I am, though," I said.

"You're probably right. I knew that I couldn't just go on making a pest of myself at the inn forever, and of course I'm glad that your father and I have finally been able to come together like this, but somehow I just can't forget the feeling of living in a group with so many other people. It's in me even now, an unending presence deep within me, like the crashing of the sea."

Having said this, my mother pressed her hand to her mouth and slipped into a little fit of giggles. "My," she said, "aren't I the poet today!"

I was still terribly young at the time, so my memory of this is a little vague, but there was a routine we used to go through every so often that makes me smile when I think of it now. Often during the summer I would get so worn out from playing all day that after dinner I would just flop down next to the low table where we ate and lie there watching TV. Soon I would begin drifting off to sleep, and my mother and father would start talking about their problems, and then I would make the mistake of waking up. I'd end up lying there with my eyes half open, gazing at the tatami from about as close up as it's possible to get, listening to them talk. As a matter of fact, this happened fairly often. My father would keep going on and on and on about how his wife in Tokyo just wouldn't agree to the divorce, and about how he couldn't bear to have the two of us spending all our time in a place like this, and about anything and everything else that came to mind. Back when he was younger he was always agonizing over things like that, always taking the gloomiest view. That's the kind of person he was then. It was only after he met my mother that he began to correct that aspect of his personality. And I really think he's changed a lot. After all, my mother is a very optimistic person.

I remember her response to my father during the particular conversation I'm thinking of. "A place like this?" she said. "That's a rude thing to say!"

"Sorry, sorry. I didn't mean it, I just got carried away. Of course Masako is your sister; there's no denying that. But still, you're mooching off these folks and you spend all day every day doing backbreaking work—you call that being happy?" Once again my father launched into an interminable speech. Even lying there with my back to the two of them I could sense that my mother was starting to get annoyed. She hates having to listen to people complain.

"All right, enough!" she said finally, heaving a profound sigh. I can still remember these words perfectly. As a matter of fact, this sentence always used to drift up into my head whenever things got rough—that's how strong an impression it made. "If you spend your time talking like that, you'll just end up complaining forever! You'll be moaning that something's missing even as they lay you out in your coffin. I don't want to hear it anymore, okay?"

And then there was that time with Tsugumi.

We were in her room one day, making a tape of some record. "Man, your dad sure takes the cake, doesn't he? He's extraordinary, he really is," she murmured, a kind of meditative shadow in her voice. It was a cloudy afternoon. One of those days when the weather outside is heavy and gray, and the waves look sharp and dangerously steep. On days like this Tsugumi always acts just a tiny bit friendlier toward the people around her. Aunt Masako once said that she thought maybe this was because on a day like this, back when Tsugumi was still a baby, she had come extremely close to dying.

"What do you mean?" I asked. "Ordinary in what way?"

"Moron! I said extraordinary, not extra ordinary! And I even meant the cake bit literally. I bet he ate nothing but sweets when

46

he was a kid. He must have had the most cushy childhood imaginable! That's what I mean when I say he's extraordinary. The guy should have been born a prince. You see? Catch my drift, darling?" Tsugumi smirked up at me from her futon. She was running a slight fever then, and her cheeks were glowing. Her hair lay fanned out over the pristine white pillowcase.

"Yeah, he does seem that way. But what made you think that?"

"Come on, he's always fussing about these things that are really no big deal, right? And even though he's a major wimp, he's always acting so high and mighty, you know—just like you, in fact, except that even you aren't as much of a wuss as your dad. I don't know, it seems to me like the man has some kind of problem dealing with reality."

To a certain extent what Tsugumi said really was true, so I found it hard to get angry at her. "Whatever, my father's just fine the way he is," I said. "Besides, isn't that why he and my mom get along so well?"

"Yeah, probably. Anyway, someone like your dad is a hell of a lot easier to warm up to than a futonridden martyr like me. A lot better than a girl who's learned everything she knows lying on her back on a futon, huh? Sounds a bit dirty when you say it that way, I guess? Heh heh. But you know, sometimes I run into your old man in the hall, right, and he says, *Hey Tsugumi, anything you want from Tokyo? Just let me know and I'll bring it when I come!* And I gotta tell you, babe, when he pulls that kind of trick even I start beaming."

Tsugumi looked at me and laughed. Mixed in with the afternoon light that flooded the room, the glow of the reading lamp looked incredibly white. A string of melodies flowed quietly on and on in the background. We sat in silence until the record ended, listening to this music, reading our magazines. Then the room was enveloped in a blanket of stillness that was disturbed only at intervals by the quiet rustle of pages flipping, flipping, flipping.

Tsugumi.

I understand her now that I'm so far away.

She did everything in her power to maintain that nasty front for no other reason than to prevent people from understanding her—I can see that now. (Of course there's no denying that she had good material to work with.) And it seems to me that even though I'm the one who is supposedly able to meet anyone and go anywhere I want in the world, and even though she remains stuck there in that little nothing of a town, I'm the one who's being forgotten by her, not the other way around. Because Tsugumi never turns her gaze back to the past. Because for Tsugumi there is only *today*.

The telephone rang one night, and when I picked up the receiver and said hello, Tsugumi's voice came over the line. "Hey, babe, it's me."

All of a sudden the light and the shadows of that old town seemed to rise up before me. The space before my eyes went totally white.

"Oh my God!" I cried. "How are you, Tsugumi! It's so great to hear your voice again! Is everyone there doing okay?"

"Evidently you're still a total ditz, huh? Tell me, Maria, are you keeping up with your studies all right?" Tsugumi chuckled. When we got to talking like this, it felt as if the distance between us had shrunk in a blink to almost nothing. Once again we were as close as your average cousins are.

"Yeah, I'm studying all right."

"Your old man isn't having a fling with some girlie, is he? They say that when stuff like that happens twice it'll happen a third time, you know."

"Sorry to disappoint you, but he's not."

"No? Well anyway, I think the old hag on this end is gonna give your ma some kind of formal notification later on, but the word is that we're closing down the inn next spring."

"What! You mean it'll be gone?" I cried, startled.

"You got it, kid. I don't know what the hell he's thinking, but my pop says he wants to start one of those fancy European-style pensions. Manage it with some friend of theirs who's got the land. Says it's always been his dream. A dream like that just makes you want to laugh, doesn't it? Sheesh. Straight out of fairy-land. Eventually they're gonna hand the pension over to Yōko. So that's it, that's the plan."

"Are you going with them?"

"Maria babe, I can die in the mountains just as well as I can die by the sea," said Tsugumi. Her tone made it sound as if she really didn't care.

"Wow, it makes me feel lonely just thinking about it. The end of the Yamamoto Inn," I murmured. The strength had drained from my body. Somehow I'd always assumed that they would live in that town forever.

"Anyway, the point is that you'll just be bumming around this summer anyway, right? So why not come on down? The old hag says she'll put you in one of the guest rooms and stuff you with the best sashimi there is."

"I'll come. Of course I'll come!"

Like a series of projections from an old roll of 8 mm film, its colors faded, images of the town and the inside of the inn flashed through my mind. I saw Tsugumi lying there in that small room I knew so well, her skinny arm holding up the telephone receiver.

"Right, that's that then. We'll be waiting. Ah . . . hold on, the old hag is hollering at me that she'll beat me up if I don't let her talk to your mom. She's just come up the stairs. Well, talk to you later," Tsugumi said, speaking very rapidly. I said that I would get my mother, and called her to the phone.

And so it was decided. I'd spend one last summer at the inn.

Outsiders

Why was it? I wonder.

As the ferry approached the harbor I would always start to feel a little bit like an outsider, even when I was small.

Back when I was still living in the town, and I'd just taken the ferry out on some little trip and was riding it back—even then I used to have this feeling. For some reason I always felt as if I had actually come from somewhere else, and that one day I was bound to leave this harbor behind.

I guess when you're out on the ocean and you see the piers way off in the distance, shrouded in mist, you understand this very clearly: No matter where you are, you're always a bit on your own, always an outsider.

It was already late in the afternoon.

The waves sparkled so brightly in the glow of the setting sun that the glare was almost blinding, and across that water and beyond the orange sky it was just possible to make out the wharf, tiny and uncertain as a mirage. Now the music that played whenever the boat arrived at a stop started blaring out over the ancient speakers, and the captain called out the name of my old town—the town where I had grown up. Outside it was probably still hot, but here in the cabin the air-conditioning was on way too high, and it felt cold.

Earlier I had been so hyper I could hardly sit still, but once I changed from the bullet train to the high-speed ferry the seesawing of the waves had lulled me into an unintended nap, and when I woke up the excitement had faded. Still dull with sleep, I sat up a little and gazed out through the saltwater spray that covered the windows at the distant line of the shore. The familiar, well-loved beach zoomed closer and closer, like a movie sped up.

The whistle blew and then the boat swung into a wide curve and cut around the tip of the concrete wharf. As the harbor neared I caught sight of Tsugumi leaning up against the billboard there, just under the word WELCOME, her arms crossed. She was wearing a white dress.

The boat kept gliding slowly forward, then bumped to a halt. Members of the crew tossed out the ropes and set out the gangway. Passenger after passenger stepped down out of the cabin into the pale twilight outside. I stood up and gathered my luggage, then went to join the line of people waiting to disembark.

One step out of the cabin and the heat was stifling. Tsugumi marched straight over to where I was standing, and without so much as a "Long time no see!" or a "How've you been?"—and still scowling—she growled, "You're late."

"You haven't changed at all, I see," I said.

"Man, I was about to shrivel up," she replied, still without a hint of a smile on her face. She spun around and started striding away. I didn't say anything, but it was such a characteristically

Tsugumi-esque welcome that a glad sort of hilarity too strong to contain surged up within me, and I grinned.

The Yamamoto Inn stood where it always had. It was so perfectly the same, so solidly *there* that I started to feel strange as soon as I saw it. Everything seemed slightly out of whack, as if I had stumbled across some house that I'd visited long ago in a dream.

But the moment Tsugumi yelled into the wide-open front door of the inn that "The ugly freeloader has arrived!" things felt real again.

Pooch started barking around back, and Aunt Masako walked out grinning from the back of the building, saying, "Tsugumi, that's not a very nice thing to say!" Yōko came out as well, her face beaming, and greeted me with a bright "Hi, Maria, long time no see!" All at once everything came rushing back to me, and I started to feel a kind of bubbly sense of anticipation.

The numerous pairs of beach sandals lined up in the entryway showed how busy this final summer was going to be. The first whiff I got of the familiar scent of the house brought back my sense of the rhythm of life at the inn.

"Aunt Masako, is there anything I can do to help?" I asked.

"No, no, don't be silly. Why don't you just go inside and have a cup of tea with Yōko or something." She smiled at me, then hurried off in the direction of the kitchen, into the ruckus of busy noises emerging from it.

Come to think of it, we were just moving into that period of time in the Yamamoto Inn schedule when Yōko always sat down to eat before she left for work. It was the busiest hour of the whole day, the time when my aunt and uncle hurled themselves into the labor of getting dinner to the guests. In the world of the inn, each day passed in the same flow of time.

Going inside, I found Yōko just starting to eat a few onigiri—balls of rice in seaweed. She took out the cup I'd always used and set it down on the low table, then poured some tea into it. "Here you go," she said, pushing the cup toward me. Her eyes were bright, and her face wore a wide, delighted smile. "Do you want one of these onigiri?"

"Hey, asshole! The girl's about to sit down to a feast. You really want her to spoil her dinner with that crap?" Tsugumi was slumped back against the wall over in a corner of the room, her legs sticking straight out. She was leafing through a magazine, and she hadn't even looked up when she spoke.

"That's true, isn't it? Well, I'll bring home some cakes tonight, then, okay? That's something to look forward to, right?" said Yōko.

"I take it you've been working at that place all along?"

"Yup. Oh, but we're selling some new kinds of cake now! I'll bring home some of the new ones tonight so you can try them."

"Sounds great!" I said.

The windows were open, and guests returning to the inn after a swim in the ocean sauntered by just outside the screens, their laughter echoing cheerfully back and forth. By now the dinner hour had begun at all the inns, and the whole town was alive. The sky was still light, and the sound of the evening news was streaming from the TV. The fragrance of the sea breeze swished across the tatami and whirled through the room. Out in the hall, hurried footsteps skittered up and down, and groups of guests heading back to their rooms after a soak in the inn's spas ambled by, filling the air around them with clouds of noise. Way off in the distance you could just make out the cries of seagulls over the water, and when you tilted your head up to look out the window, a sky so wildly crimson it was almost frightening glowed between the power lines. It was an evening exactly like all the others.

Even so, I was aware that nothing lasts forever.

We heard a man's voice asking if Maria had arrived yet and then footsteps coming down the hall toward the room, and suddenly my uncle stuck his head in under the curtain that hung in the doorway. "Hey Maria, good to see you! Make yourself at home!" He gave me a smile and went out again.

Tsugumi stood up, padded over to the refrigerator, poured some wheat tea into the Mickey Mouse glass she'd gotten way back when as a giveaway at the liquor store, and gulped the liquid down. Then she plunked the empty glass down in the well-polished sink.

"A face like that, and the guy wants to start a pension. He sure knows how to make a nuisance of himself, let me tell you," she said.

"He's always dreamed of it," said Yōko casually, lowering her eyes a tad.

All this had such a solid existence now, but next summer there would be no trace of any of it. I knew this, but there was no way I could make myself feel the truth of it. No way to make it seem real. And I bet it didn't seem real to them either.

Everyday life had never really made much of an impression on me before. I used to live here in this little fishing village. I would sleep and wake up, have meals. Sometimes I felt really great; other times I felt a little out of it. I watched TV, fell in love, went to classes at school, and at the end of every day I always came back here, to this same house. But when I let my thoughts wander back through the ordinariness of those cycles now, I find that somewhere along the way it has all acquired a touch of warmth—that I've been left with something silky and dry and warm, like clean sand.

Soaking up that gentle heat, a little tired from all the hustle and bustle of travel, I let myself savor an enticingly familiar sense of happiness.

Summer was coming. Yes, summer was about to begin.

A season that would come and go only once, and never return again. All of us understood that very well, and yet we would probably just pass our days the way we always had. And this made the ticking of time feel slightly more tense than in the old days, infused it with a hint of distress. We could all feel this as we sat there that evening, together. We could feel it so clearly that it made us sad, and yet at the same time we were extremely happy.

I was pulling things out of my bags after dinner when I heard Pooch start yipping excitedly. You could see the back garden if you leaned out the small window in my room. Peering down into the twilight, I saw Tsugumi untying Pooch and hooking his leash to his collar. She noticed me and looked up.

"Hey, you wanna walk with us?" she asked.

"Sure," I said, and went downstairs.

Outside, traces of light still lingered in the sky, and against that background the streetlamps seemed to shine more clearly than usual. Tsugumi kept being yanked along by Pooch, just the same as before.

"I'm tired today, so we're only going as far as the beach," she said.

"Do you walk like this every night?" I asked, surprised. It didn't seem like the kind of thing Tsugumi was really healthy enough to be doing.

"As if I have any choice! Hell, you're the one who got the dumb mutt used to these walks. After you left he started making this unbelievable noise every morning, a whine like you can't imagine, right at the time when you used to take him out. Little Tsugumi with her delicate health was constantly getting woken up by this, you realize. So what else were we supposed to do? Yōko and I pleaded with the brute until he was gracious enough to compromise and let us take him out in the evening instead of the morning. The two of us walk him together."

"Wow, that's wonderful!"

"It does seem that getting jerked around like this by Pooch has made me a little stronger than I used to be, so it has its good points." Tsugumi's small head was turned so that I saw it in profile. She was smiling.

All her life Tsugumi has had to live with problems in one part of her body or another, but she hardly ever tells you where the pain is, not even as part of a joke. She just keeps it to herself and then takes her anger out on the people around her, or says things she knows will make everyone mad and then goes off to lie alone in her bed. And the girl never gives up.

I found this attitude kind of gallant, but sometimes it got on my nerves.

Night had almost fallen, and the street was deep blue and heavy with heat, and all along the vague white blur of the beach children were out setting off fireworks. We walked to the end of the gravel path, passed by the bridge, and headed toward the shore. We walked up to the top of the embankment that stretches straight out into the sea, and set Pooch free. While he tore off in the direction of the beach, Tsugumi and I climbed up on one of the huge concrete blocks that lined the edge of the sand and sat down, leaning back into two of its corners. Then we opened the cans of cold juice we'd just bought.

The wind felt good. Here and there the final glow of twilight would shine through holes in the thin sheet of gray clouds that hovered up there, flowing off into the distance, and then the light would blink out of sight again. And all the while the darkness went on pushing its way down the sky.

Pooch kept running off until we couldn't even see him anymore and then coming back with a worried expression on his face and barking up at Tsugumi where she sat on the breakwater, too high up for him to reach. Tsugumi would grin and stretch out her hand and pet him or else give him a whack.

"You've really gotten to be good pals with Pooch, haven't you, Tsugumi?" I said. It moved me to see that their friendship had grown even warmer since the previous summer.

Tsugumi didn't reply. As long as she kept quiet, she actually seemed like what she was—a younger cousin. But after a while she made a face like she had bitten down on a lemon, and muttered her reply.

"It's no joke, kid. This is the pits. I feel like some sort of Don Juan who's gotten himself all tangled up in the passions of one of his young virgins and accidentally ended up married."

"What are you talking about? That's supposed to be a metaphor for your friendship with Pooch?" I kind of felt like I knew what she meant, but I wanted to make her explain a little more. I figured I might as well try taking this line. And Tsugumi answered.

"You bet it is, babe! Makes me shudder to think that I've gotten this buddy-buddy with a dog. If you consider it objectively it's pretty gross, you know."

"Oh please. Is this your idea of being sheepish?" I laughed.

Tsugumi made an ironic face. "Give me a break, Maria! You really don't understand me at all, do you? I mean, how many years have you and I been together? Try using your brain every once in a while."

"No, no, I do understand. I was just teasing you," I said. "But I also know that you don't have as much of an aversion to Pooch as you pretend."

"Yeah, I guess that's true. I do like him, I like Pooch," said Tsugumi.

The dusk surrounding us was a mass of any number of colors piled one on top of the other, and everything around us seemed to hover in space, deeply blurred, as if we were in a dream. Every so often a wave would hit up against the awkward silhouette of one of the breakwater's concrete blocks, and the water would dance. The first star glittered brightly in the sky, looking like a tiny white bulb.

"But you see, nasty people have a special kind of nasty-people philosophy. This business with the mutt goes against that," Tsugumi continued. "A nasty person who gets along with dogs, for heaven's sake! It's too easy."

"A nasty person?" I grinned.

Evidently in the time since we'd last been together, some things had piled up inside Tsugumi—things that, in her own way, she really wanted to get off her chest. She talked to me of her emotions. This was the kind of thing she would only speak about with me. Ever since that incident with the haunted mailbox I'd been the only person who really understood her, and even when the things she wanted to say had no relation to the way I was living my life, I still got the message.

"Okay, imagine that there's a huge famine all across the globe."

"A famine? . . . Sorry, too far out. I can't imagine it."

"Maria, you're a pest. Just shut up and listen, okay? The idea is that I want to be the kind of jerk who could kill Pooch and eat him if it got like that—to a point where there was really nothing left to eat anymore—and not feel anything. Of course I don't mean one of these half-baked jerks who'd shed a little tear afterward and then go put up a tombstone and whisper to it, 'I'm so sorry it had to be this way, Pooch, but thanks to you maybe the rest of us will survive.' I'm not talking about the kind of person who'd take a little chip of bone and make it into a pendant and wear it wherever she went. I want to be able to just laugh and say, 'Wow, that Pooch sure was delicious!' and I want to be able to feel really calm as I say it, and if possible I don't want to feel any regret or any twinges of conscience, you see? Of course that's just an example."

The huge gap between the way Tsugumi looked as she sat there with her head slightly cocked, entranced by her own words, her skinny arms wrapped around her knees, and these things she was saying—that gap really made me feel strange. It was like I was seeing something from another world.

"I'd call that a strange person, not a nasty person," I said.

Tsugumi was staring straight out across the dark ocean. She continued to speak very calmly, in a pleasant tone. "Yeah. That's the kind of gal you just can't figure out. Something about her always seems to hold her a little apart from everyone around her, and even though she herself doesn't understand this stuff that's going on inside her she doesn't ever try to stop it, even though she has no idea where it may lead her—and yet you get the feeling that in the end she's probably right . . . That's what makes her so cool."

It wasn't narcissism. And it wasn't exactly an aesthetic. Deep down inside, Tsugumi had this perfectly polished mirror, and she only believed in the things she saw reflected there. She never even considered anything else.

That's what it was.

And yet I liked her even so, and Pooch liked her, and probably everyone else around her liked her too. We all continued to be enchanted by her. It didn't matter what she put us through, or what awful things she said to us just because she happened to be in a crummy mood. In Pooch's case, it didn't matter that he might eventually end up being killed and eaten. Beyond her words and beyond her heart, much deeper than all that, supporting the snarl of who she was, was a light so strong it made you sad. Like a machine that has achieved perpetual motion, in some place that even Tsugumi herself wasn't aware of, that light continued to shine.

"It's cold now that the sun has gone down. Wanna head back?" Tsugumi said, standing up.

"Gosh, that was unladylike! I could see your undies."

"So you see my undies, big deal. I can bear that much exposure."

"Yeah, well that doesn't mean you should *bare* it all, ha ha."

"Very funny, kid," said Tsugumi, laughing. Then she shouted for Pooch. The dog dashed back at full speed, running in a straight line down the long embankment, then started prancing around, barking vigorously, as if he were telling us about all the different things he had just done.

"Yeah, we hear you. Good boy," Tsugumi said.

We started walking. Pooch kept chasing after us and then trotting on ahead and stopping to wait. And then all of a sudden he jerked up his head as if he had noticed something, and streaked off in the same direction we were headed. I was still wondering what it was that had caught his attention when we heard him start barking his head off down on the other side of the embankment, which was evidently where he had ended up.

"What's gotten into him?" we exclaimed, and ran over to where we could see him. Pooch was bouncing about excitedly, leaping up and down around a Pomeranian that had been tied to the base of the white statue in the smallish park on the other side of the embankment. The statue is in the middle of a little stand of pines. At first Pooch had been wagging his tail, eager to play, but having a dog as enormous as Pooch come springing at him like that had totally terrified the Pomeranian, and he became desperate. Yipping furiously, he nipped at Pooch. The latter yelped and sprang away, then turned serious. A moment later he'd turned himself into a cold-blooded fighting dog.

In the same instant that I shouted out, "We've got to stop them!" Tsugumi growled, "Sic 'im, Pooch!" It was one of those moments when the difference between our two personalities was made particularly apparent.

There was nothing else to do, so I ran down alone and wrapped my arms around Pooch, using all my strength to hold him back. And then the little runt of a Pomeranian bit my ankle.

"YOW, that hurt! What was that for, you little bastard!" I shouted.

"Yeah baby! Go to it, all three of you!" cried Tsugumi.

I turned around to look at her, and saw that she was laughing. She had an expression on her face like she couldn't be more thrilled.

And then it happened.

"Hey, Gongorō! Stop it!" called a young man, striding over.

This was our first encounter with Kyōichi, the other person who would be sharing the good old days of this final summer with us. All around us was the shallow darkness of early night, and it was still early in the summer. A blue moon like a painting was just beginning to climb up over the shore.

Kyōichi certainly did make a strange impression on me. He appeared to be about the same age as us. He was tall and slender, but his shoulders and neck were thick and sturdy—a combination that made him look strong in a really cool sort of way. His hair was cut short, his eyebrows looked kind of harsh—if you just glanced at him he seemed like a pleasant, carefree young guy, just the sort of person who ought to be wearing the white polo shirt he had on. But his eyes were a little different. His gaze was strangely deep, and there was a light in them that made it seem as if he knew something huge, something extremely important. Perhaps you could say that, unlike the rest of him, his eyes were old.

He strode over to where I was still sitting, right in the middle of the storm of barking that had marked the renewal of hostilities between Pooch and Gongorō. The latter was jumping around like crazy, making an awful racket. Even so, Kyōichi scooped him up lightly and cradled him in his arms.

"Are you all right?" he said. He stood with his back perfectly straight.

Finally able to release Pooch from the powerful grasp in which I had been holding him, I stood up. "Yes, I'm fine," I said. "I'm afraid our dog came over and started meddling with yours, so it was our fault. Sorry."

"Nah, this little guy here is a fighter to start with, and what's more he isn't afraid of anything," said Kyōichi, chuckling. He turned to look at Tsugumi. "How about you, are you okay?"

Tsugumi instantly flicked the channel on her personality.

"Oh yes, thank you." She smiled shyly.

"Well then, see you around," said Kyōichi, and walked off in the direction of the beach, still holding Gongorō in his arms.

By now the night had deepened. It seemed to have plunged quickly down upon us during these last few minutes. Pooch stared up at us, as if in reproach, panting slightly through his nose.

"Let's go," Tsugumi said, and we started strolling back.

Here and there along the road the shadows of summer lay hidden. There was something sweet about the night air and the energy that surrounded us, something that seemed to infuse the evening with an excited vigor. You felt as if it colored even the fragrance of the breeze. The people we passed were all full of spirit and very boisterous. Everyone seemed to be having a blast.

"We should get home just about the same time that Yōko comes with the cakes, don't you think?" I said, having completely forgotten the business with the dogs.

"Yeah, and you guys can do what you like with them. You oughta know how I feel about the foul cakes they make at that place," replied Tsugumi. Her tone was a little vacant, and I decided to take advantage of this to tease her.

"I bet you've got your eye on that guy, right?" I said.

But Tsugumi wasn't at all ruffled by my comment.

"He sure was something, wasn't he?" she murmured.

Did she have some kind of premonition then?

"What do you mean? In what way?"

I hadn't felt anything special when we were with him, so I repeated this question several times, trying to figure out what she meant. But Tsugumi didn't answer. She just kept walking silently along the dark road with Pooch at her side.

Of the Night

Every so often I'll have one of these really bizarre nights.

Nights when space itself seems to have shifted a little out of line, and I feel as if I'm on the verge of seeing everything all at once. I lie there in my futon, unable to fall asleep, listening to that clock up there on the wall, and the ticking of the second hand and the rays of moonlight that stream across the ceiling dominate the night, just like they did when I was a little girl. *This night will go on forever.* And yet it seems that back then nights used to be even longer than this—ever so much longer. I catch a faint whiff of some unknown scent. Perhaps it's the scent of saying goodbye, so faint it seems slightly sweet.

There was a night like this years ago that I'll never forget.

I was in one of the upper grades of elementary school. Tsugumi and Yōko and I had gotten completely caught up in some program on TV. We were so passionate about it that it was as if we had all come down with some kind of fever. It was about this girl who went around having all kinds of adventures as she searched for her little sister. Tsugumi didn't usually fall for overblown gags like that, but this time even she kept coming week after week to watch it with Yōko and me, never missing an episode. It's odd, but my impressions of the program itself have faded, become lost in a shroud of mist, and all that comes back to me is the feeling of what it was like to watch it—an excited memory of the thrill we felt. The lighting in the TV room, the flavor of the Calpis drink we always had when we watched this show, the vaguely warm breeze that blew out from the fan—all this comes together again inside me just the way it was, vividly real. Watching this show was one of the high points in our week. And then one night we found ourselves confronted with the fact that we had just finished watching the end of the last episode in the series.

At dinner we were all very quiet.

Aunt Masako chuckled. "Oh, I see! That program you all like so much finished tonight. That's it, isn't it?" she said.

Tsugumi, who had been going through her rebellious teens ever since she was born, growled back, "Keep your mouth shut unless you've got something worth saying!"

Yōko and I were feeling pretty down too, and though neither of us was in any sort of rebellious period, for once we kind of felt that Tsugumi's response had hit the mark. I guess this shows how much we loved the program.

That night, having wriggled down into my futon all alone, I found myself in the grips of a wrenching sadness. I was only a child, but I knew the feeling that came when you parted with something, and I felt that pain. I lay gazing up at the ceiling, feeling the sleek stiffness of the well-starched sheets against my skin. My distress was a seed that would grow into an understanding of what it means to say goodbye. In contrast to the heavy ache I would come to know later on in life, this was tiny and fresh—a green bud of pain with a bright halo of light rimming its edges. Unable to sleep, I got up and wandered out into the hall. It was pitch black, and the clock on the wall was *tick-tick-ticking* with the same loud noise as always. The white of the paper that covered the sliding doors seemed to hover there in the dark, vague and dim, and I felt terribly small. I kept remembering scenes from the show—after all, it had been the center of my life for quite a while now; I'd been so absorbed in it that I'd totally forgotten everything else. The night was still enough that I didn't want to go back into my room, and I inched my way down the stairs, one barefoot step at a time. I wanted to breathe some fresh air, so I went out into the garden. It was flooded with moonlight, and the hulking silhouettes of the trees stood there quietly, holding their breath.

"Hey, Maria!" Yōko called out suddenly, but somehow I didn't feel a bit surprised. She was standing there in the garden, dressed in her pajamas. "You couldn't sleep either?" she whispered. The faint glow of the moon lit her face.

"Nope," I said, keeping my voice down too.

"Same for both of us," Yōko said. Her long hair was braided, and she was bent over, running her fingers along the spiraling vine of a morning glory.

"Want to go for a walk?" I asked her. "Though I guess we would get yelled at if anyone found out. Were you very quiet when you came out?"

"Yeah, I was. You don't have to worry about that."

The gate whined quietly as we pushed it open. Suddenly the aroma of the tide drifting through the darkness seemed to grow stronger.

"Finally we don't have to be quiet anymore."

"Yeah. It feels great out tonight, doesn't it?"

Yōko was in pajamas, I was in a thin cotton kimono. I had on my sandals and I wasn't wearing any socks, but I kept walking on toward the ocean anyway, just as I was. The moon had climbed up high overhead. A line of fishing boats stood along the edge of the road that led up to the peak of the mountain, all of them sunk in such a profound sleep that you would think they were just rotting away. This wasn't the town we knew. It felt as if we had arrived someplace unrecognizable, fantastically distant from everyday life.

All of a sudden, Yōko spoke. "Who would ever have guessed that I would find my sister here, of all places!" she cried.

At first I thought she was just taking on the role of the main character in the TV show again, but after a moment I realized that it was real. Tsugumi was crouched down all alone at the very end of the path that led to the beach, gazing out over the ocean.

"You dimwits came too?" Tsugumi said, her tone quieter than ever. The way she spoke, it sounded as if she found it perfectly natural that we were there, almost as if we had arranged to meet in advance. She briskly rose to her feet and stood there, a wall of darkness at her back.

"Tsugumi, you're barefoot!" cried Yōko.

Yōko stripped off her socks and gave them to Tsugumi. Tsugumi fooled around for a while, putting them on her hands and saying, "Hmm, is this right?" and stuff like that, but when we totally ignored her she slipped her shockingly bony feet into them and started walking.

Through rays of moonlight.

"Maybe walk around the harbor once and head home?" said Yōko.

"Sure. We can get some sodas before turning back," I agreed.
But Tsugumi disagreed. "Suit yourself. I've got other plans."
"Why? What are you going to do?" I asked.

She replied clearly, not looking at me. "I'm going to walk."
"Walk where? How far?"

"As far as the next beach, right across the mountain."

"Doesn't that sound kind of dangerous?" said Yōko. Then,
"Though to tell the truth, I wouldn't mind giving it a try myself."

There was no one else on the road that climbed the mountain,
and it was as black as a cave. The high bluff that bordered the road
cut off the moonlight, plunging us into shadow, and we had a hard
time just making out the ground beneath our feet. Yōko and I held
hands and walked on carefully through this blind world, as if groping our way through the dark. Tsugumi strode rapidly on by herself, a little bit off to the side, keeping in line with the two of us.
Her footsteps were so steady and sure that I remember looking at
her and finding it hard to believe she was actually walking in the
dark like us. The darkness was frightening.

We had come out on this walk as a way to deal with our sadness, to mourn the end of our favorite TV program. But we had
totally forgotten that now, and as we trekked over the peak of
the mountain, deep in the heart of night, surrounded by the wind
shaking through clusters of trees, we felt a sort of eager excitement. As we made our way farther and farther down the slope
of the mountain, the neighboring town, a small fishing village,
appeared before us under the dark cover of midnight. Before long
the beach came into view.

The rocky shore was lined with little stands and shops that
only stayed open for the summer. They were all boarded up,
with an aura of emptiness about them that made you think of

ghosts. Way out in the water the flags on the buoys were swaying vigorously back and forth, in time with the roar of the waves.
The slight nip in the wind cooled our burning cheeks. We all
bought sodas. The clunking of the vending machine in the night
seemed to send a shiver of surprise across the entire pitch-black
expanse of the beach. The dark ocean undulated before us, blank
and vague. Way off in the distance, the lights of our town glittered faintly, like a mirage.

"It's like the afterlife or something, huh?" Tsugumi said.

Yōko and I nodded, murmuring our agreement.

A little later we started back along the same mountain road
we'd come by, and arrived back at the Yamamoto Inn completely
worn out. We wished each other a good night and then slipped
off to our own rooms and slept so soundly that we might as well
have been dead.

The hardest part came the next morning. At breakfast Yōko
and I were so exhausted that we couldn't even make conversation.
The two of us just sat there in silence, rubbing our tired eyes,
chewing our food. Compared to the way we'd been the previous
night, alive with that strange energy, we might as well have been
different people altogether. Tsugumi didn't even get up.

There's something else I know about that night.

Tsugumi had picked up a white stone while we were out on
the beach and taken it with her, and even now it was sitting there
in one of the corners of her bookshelf. I really have no idea what
Tsugumi was feeling that night. I don't know what sort of emotions that rock held for her. Maybe it wasn't anything special at
all, maybe she just scooped it up on a whim. And yet whenever
I find myself starting to forget that *Tsugumi belongs to life,* I always think of that stone, of her feeling such an overwhelming

urge to walk that she went outside without even putting on her sandals, and every time I remember these things I start to feel sort of sad, and my mind gets very sharp and clear, and I think things through in a very levelheaded way.

For some reason I was thinking about all this again. Glancing over at the clock, I saw that it was nearly two. The thoughts people have when they can't get to sleep are generally a little weird. Your mind rambles through the dark, tossing up one dreamy conclusion after another, each one as tender as a bubble. All of a sudden I realized that sometime after that night, at some unknowable point along the way, I had grown up. I wasn't living here in this town now, not anymore, I was attending a university in Tokyo. It all seemed so bizarre. My hands lay stretched out in the darkness, and somehow they didn't seem to belong to me.

Suddenly the door to my room slid open.

"Hey, get up!" barked Tsugumi.

She had given me a terrible start, and my pounding heart refused to quiet. It took a few moments before I finally managed to speak.

"What do you want?"

Tsugumi sashayed into my room as boldly as if it were hers, and crouched down by my pillow. "I can't sleep."

I was staying in the room right next to Tsugumi's, so I should probably just have considered myself lucky that this kind of thing hadn't happened before. I squirmed about in my futon for a bit and sat up.

"Yeah, well is that my fault?" I said testily.

"Oh, don't be so grumpy. Think of it as some kind of karma and help me think up something fun to do. C'mon, be a pal!" Tsugumi grinned.

It's only at times like this that Tsugumi assumes this docile attitude, letting you feel as if you're in control. All at once I found myself remembering the numerous occasions when she had barged in and woken me up with a whack, and how she used to stomp on my hands or feet when I was sleeping, and how she would go in and sneak the dictionary out of my desk while I was in gym class simply because she didn't feel like bringing her own to school—she claimed it was too heavy! One little dictionary!—and all sorts of other pranks like that. Suddenly I was in the midst of a flashback, a familiar sense of irritation at the unreasonableness of it all, and what I remembered gave me a shock. How on earth could I have forgotten? My relationship with Tsugumi was certainly no endless party.

"Listen, Tsugumi, I'm tired," I said. I wanted to try putting up a little bit of resistance, just a little, the way I had in the old days. But at moments like this Tsugumi never listened to a word anyone said.

"Hey, it's the same, isn't it?" Tsugumi asked, her eyes glittering.

"The same as what?"

"Man, you know what I'm talking about! That night when the three of us went over to the next town, like total idiots. It was just this time of the year. Same season, something about the night that keeps you from getting to sleep. Yōko's in there snoring her brains out, but she never picks up on these things. She must be the dullest person on the face of the globe."

"As a matter of fact I was just about to fall asleep myself."

"It's your fault for staying in this room. You knew I was next door."

"What else am I supposed to do, Tsugumi?" I sighed. But to

tell the truth, the feeling I had then was pretty good. It all seemed so strange. After all, she and I had been having precisely the same thoughts—it was like telepathy, our minds linking through the night. Every so often night plays these little tricks. A knot of air pushes quietly through the darkness, and a feeling that has converged in some far-off place tumbles down like a falling star and lands just in front of you, and then you wake up. Two people live the same dream. All this takes place in the space of a single night, and the feeling only lasts until morning. The next morning it gets lost in the light, and you're no longer even sure it happened. But nights like this are long. They continue forever, glittering like a jewel.

"All right, then, you want to go for a walk?" I asked.

"Hmm . . . Nah, I don't have the energy for that," Tsugumi replied.

"Well, what do you want to do?"

"You expect me to think through details like that?"

"I wish you would before you wake me up!"

"All right, babe, I got it," Tsugumi said. "Let's just get some drinks out of your fridge and go out on the veranda. It's not great, but I'll deal."

I stood up and went over to the refrigerator. The room I'd been given was actually meant for paying guests, so there were plenty of drinks. I took out a beer for myself and tossed Tsugumi a can of orange juice. She can't handle any alcohol at all, and no one ever lets her try because every time she does she ends up barfing all over the place.

We tiptoed down the hall just like we used to in the old days, holding our breath, then quietly opened the door and stepped out onto the veranda. This is where the poles for drying laundry were, and during the daytime there were always lines of towels flapping in the wind, like in a commercial for detergent. The nighttime was different, though—the veranda was empty, with nothing but rows of bare poles. They were rather hefty poles. In between them you could see the stars. The veranda looked out on the mountains, whose heavy green silhouettes seemed to loom toward you, filling your eyes.

I took a swallow of beer. It was very cold, and the liquid seemed to burrow right down to the pit of my chest. The chill I felt was an echo of the night.

Tsugumi took a sip of her juice, too.

"Why do drinks taste so good outside like this, at night?" she murmured.

"Things like that are important to you, aren't they, Tsugumi?" I asked.

But without even asking what I meant, Tsugumi grunted, "Like hell they are!"

I hadn't said I was talking about her emotions—it was a matter of sensibility. A few moments of thoughtful silence passed before Tsugumi continued.

"I may be the sort of chick who'd just get irritated looking at the last leaf on the plant in that O. Henry story, and rip it off, but I'm able to see the beauty in it. Is that what you mean?"

Her reply left me a bit taken aback. "You know, Tsugumi, I get the feeling that you've started speaking more like a human being lately," I said.

"Maybe my time is running out." Tsugumi laughed.

No, that wasn't it. It was because of this night.

On nights like this when the air is so clear, you end up saying things you ordinarily wouldn't. Without even noticing what you're doing, you open up your heart and just start talking to the person next to you—you talk as if you have no audience but the glittering stars, far overhead. There are any number of negatives showing nights like this filed in the "Summer Nights" section of my brain. *I suppose this night we're enjoying now, out here on this veranda, will end up tucked away someplace very close to the page for that night when the three of us were young and we just kept walking on and on . . .* The knowledge that as long as I went on living I would always have chances to feel these nights made it possible for me to have hope for the future. Lovely nights like tonight. The wonderful scent of the wind—a fragrance reminiscent of the aura of the mountains and the sea, which weaves slowly, translucently through every little nook and cranny of our town. I knew this night would never be back, but that didn't matter. Just having the possibility, just knowing that I might find myself again in a night like this, in some other summer, was enough to make it all perfect.

Tsugumi had finished drinking her juice. She leapt up nimbly, making a fast, whooshy sort of standing-up noise, and padded over to the railing, where she could look down on the street.

"Not a soul in sight," she said.

"Hey, Tsugumi?" I asked. "What's that building over there?"

Over at the base of the mountain you could see this really giant building, a little bit of the iron scaffolding still visible at the top, and I'd been wondering about it for some time. Even now, with the whole town plunged in darkness, it stood out from the lines of buildings around it.

"You mean that? It's a hotel," Tsugumi replied, glancing back at me.

"They're putting up a new hotel? A place that big?"

"You got it, babe. I kind of figure that must be part of the reason the old pa and ma decided to shut down the inn. Not that I give a damn what happens to the lousy wreck or anything, but when you get right down to it it's a matter of life and death for us, isn't it? Of course my father gets to make this bold new start and all, do what he's always wanted to do with his life, that kind of thing, so maybe there's no problem, huh? Be sad when the elegant pension goes bust and the four of us end up committing suicide together off in the rugged wilds of the mountains, of course. Nothing left but our skeletons sprawled out in the dirt somewhere, picked clean by wild beasts and bleached by the rain. What a tragedy."

"No, you'll do all right. I'll come and stay with you every year. And if I ever get married, I'll come have the ceremony at the pension."

"You know what, Maria? Instead of annoying people with these god-awful, hackneyed-as-hell dreams of yours, why don't you try bringing some college girls along sometime? We don't get them here. The species doesn't exist."

"What about Yōko?"

"She doesn't count. I want someone a little more hip. I mean, the only time I've ever even seen chicks like that is on TV," Tsugumi said, flopping her sandals around as she spoke. "I want to have a chance to look a few over and come up with all kinds of nasty things to say about them."

Not counting all the times when she'd had to go visit some hospital or other, Tsugumi had grown up almost without having left the town. It really hurt to think about that.

I stood up and went over to stand by Tsugumi.

"You should come visit me in Tokyo," I said, staring down over the railing. The narrow alley below us was very still, and sunk in shadow.

"Yeah, maybe. But I don't know . . . you remember that book *Heidi* we read when we were kids? I'd feel kinda like that friend of hers with the bad leg." Tsugumi chuckled sheepishly.

"Literary classics seems to be the topic of the day." I laughed.

Just then, I spotted a familiar-looking dog trotting along the road that passes by the front of the inn. I shouted. "Oh my God! That was what's-his-name! Gonnosuke! . . . no, that's not right . . . That dog from the other day!"

Tsugumi leaned out over the railing. "It's Gongorō!" she cried. Then, in a voice so thunderous that it reverberated down the dark street, she hollered, "Hey Gongorō!" Far away I heard the sound of Pooch waking up and moving around, shaking his chain. It was the first time in ages that I'd seen Tsugumi behave in such an uncool way, and I was shocked.

Had Tsugumi's passion actually reached that runt of a dog?

Gongorō came padding back along the dark road. He stood there for a few moments looking this way and that, trying to figure out where that shout he'd heard had come from. He was really funny to watch, and I was still laughing when I called his name. This time he seemed to have located us all right, and he stood peering up at us, yipping.

"Hey, who is that?"

For a moment I had the impression that Gongorō had spoken. And then all of a sudden, as if he were walking into the beam of a spotlight, the guy we'd run into at the park a few days earlier stepped into the glow of a streetlamp. He was much more tanned than he had been the first time we saw him. His black T-shirt seemed to merge with the surrounding dark.

"Oh, it's you two."

"Tsugumi, isn't this great! It's him!" I whispered.

"Yeah, thanks. I noticed," she replied. Then she hollered into the street, "Hey moron, what do you call yourself? You got some kind of name?"

The guy scooped up Gongorō and looked up at us.

"My name's Kyōichi. What about you two?"

"I'm Tsugumi. This here's Maria. Tell me, whose kid are you?"

"I'm not living in this town yet, but I'll be over that way," he said, pointing toward the mountains. "That new hotel is gonna be my house."

"What, is your mother a maid or something?" Tsugumi chuckled. The smile on her face was so brilliant it almost seemed to light up the darkness.

"As a matter of fact I'm the owner's son. My parents like it here, so they want to come live in town. I'm going to college over in M., so I'll come live with them and commute to school."

Nighttime turns people into friends in next to no time. Kyōichi gave the two of us a completely relaxed, openhearted smile.

"Do you go for walks every night?" I asked.

"Nah. I don't know what it was, but somehow I just couldn't get to sleep. Gongorō was out like a log, but I got him up and made him come out with me. Poor little guy." Kyōichi grinned.

The sense that the three of us were becoming friends seemed to saturate the air between us like a kind of instinct, a pleasurable premonition. People who are going to get along really well know it almost as soon as they meet. You spend a little while talking and everyone starts to feel this conviction, you're all equally sure that you're at the beginning of something good. That's how it is when you meet people you're going to be with for a long time.

"Hey Kyōichi," said Tsugumi, her eyes bulging so much that it looked like they were going to jump out of their sockets. "I've been wanting to see you ever since that time in the park. We gonna get together again? Huh?"

I was pretty shocked by her words myself, but Kyōichi seemed totally floored. He stood there silently for a few moments before replying.

". . . Well, yeah. I mean, I'll be here all summer. I'm always wandering around town, taking Gongorō out on walks. I'm staying in Nakahama Inn. You know where that is?"

"Yeah, I know it."

"You're welcome to come visit anytime. My last name's Takeuchi."

"Gotcha." Tsugumi nodded.

"Well, catch you later."

"Good night."

Tsugumi's ardor had set the darkness on edge, but the moment Kyōichi had vanished down the dark road, the tension dispersed. It was a strange meeting. He showed up suddenly, then just as suddenly disappeared.

The night that enveloped us kept growing deeper and thicker.

"Wow, Tsugumi, you sure seem to have fallen for him!" I grinned.

"For the time being, yeah," Tsugumi replied with a sigh.

"I mean, that was so weird. Didn't you notice?"

"What do you mean? What was so weird?"

"You were talking just like you always do."

I'd been aware of it all along, but I hadn't said anything. Tsugumi always switches back into her Normal Young Woman mode in front of guys, but in talking to Kyōichi she had used the same vulgar tone she always uses. It was so intriguingly odd that I had gotten kind of jittery myself.

"Oh man!" cried Tsugumi.

"What's the problem?"

"I didn't even notice! Damn, it's true, isn't it?" she groaned. "I wasn't paying any attention to what I was doing. Man, of all the crappy mistakes! I must have sounded like some kind of nasty, foul-mouthed broad. Damn!"

"Oh, I don't know. I mean, it was . . . interesting," I said.

Tsugumi was staring straight ahead, her eyebrows tightly pinched together. The night wind puffed across her face. "Whatever, it's too late to worry now. It's all because of this night, that's what it is," she replied.

Confession

It had been raining since morning. A salt-scented summer rain.

And I was bored. I'd been holed up in my room for hours, reading.

Tsugumi had been laid up in her futon for a few days now with a fever and a terrible headache, probably as a result of our wild night out on the veranda. A little earlier, when I'd taken her lunch in to her, she'd been scrunched up in her futon, moaning. I was so used to seeing her that way that I even started to feel a bit nostalgic.

"Hey, I'll leave your lunch here for you, okay?" I shouted, setting the tray down next to her pillow. Then suddenly, as I started out the door, I came out with this: "Hey Tsugumi, do you think maybe you're just lovesick?"

Without saying a word Tsugumi whipped out her arm and hurled a nearby plastic pitcher at me.

Whatever else was wrong, that part of her was doing fine.

The pitcher slammed into the wooden post that served as a stopper for the sliding door, then tumbled across the tatami.

Thanks to this, my hair was still glistening with moisture even now. I had returned to my own room, and I was lying down with my hair fanned out peacefully across the floor.

Outside the window, way off in the distance, I could see the ocean. It was a deep gray, and the tossing waves were so wild and jagged that it was actually sort of scary to look at. The whole vast expanse of sky and ocean stood on the other side of a monotone filter of mist. On a day like today, even Pooch was probably just sitting forlornly in his doghouse, closed in by the scent of damp earth, gazing out into the rain. The guests at the inn couldn't go out to swim, and so for some time now I'd been hearing the sounds of voices downstairs, and people clumping from room to room. It was always like this when it rained. In the big house that this inn was, you ended up having too much free time on your hands. No doubt crowds of people had collected in front of the big TV in the lobby and around the ancient video game machines.

I managed to read quite a lot in the intervals when I stopped letting my lazy thoughts take control. Time and time again, images of the raindrops that kept streaming like shooting stars across the windowpane glimmered across the movie screen inside my head.

And then suddenly I had a thought.

What if Tsugumi gets worse and dies?

This fear had lived inside me ever since I was a little kid, when Tsugumi was even weaker than she was now. The possibility had always been terribly real to me. And it was something that was always jumping into my head just when I least expected it. On rainy days like this both the past and the future dissolve quietly into the air and hover there, surrounding you.

A single teardrop fell onto my open book. Before I even understood what was happening, tears were streaming from my eyes.

In the midst of my surprise, I heard the pattering of the rain as it soaked the eaves. *Maria, what's gotten into you?* I thought, wiping away my tears. And soon I'd forgotten that this had ever happened. I was just reading my book.

Around three in the afternoon I finally ran out of things to read. Tsugumi was tucked up in her futon for reasons already stated, and Yōko had gone out, and there was nothing good on TV, so I decided to fight the excess of boredom by making a trip to the bookstore. Tsugumi must have heard me sliding the door open on my way out, because she yelled at me through her closed door.

"Hey, where are you going?"

"To the bookstore. Do you want anything?" I replied.

"Get me some apple juice, will you? That 100% All Natural stuff."

Her voice was hoarse. Her fever was probably pretty high.

"Okay, I'll get some."

"And get one of those expensive melons, and some sushi, and . . ."

She kept talking, but I ignored her and went downstairs.

I get the feeling that in towns near the sea the rain falls in a more hushed, lonely way than in other places. Perhaps the ocean absorbs the sound? When I moved to Tokyo, the exaggerated roar of the rain there was one of the things that surprised me most.

I took a road parallel to the shore on my way to the bookstore. The beach had been dyed completely black by the rain, and it was as still and peaceful as a graveyard—it felt weird to see it like that. The rain falling on the water broke into the roaring waves, sending out thousands upon thousands of ripples.

The biggest bookstore in town was unbelievably crowded. Not that I was surprised or anything—on days like this all the tourists in town make a beeline for the place. A quick glance around the premises confirmed what I had suspected: All the magazines I wanted were sold out.

I had no choice but to go look through the shelves of aging paperbacks, and that's just what I was doing when I noticed— *Hey, that's Kyōichi back there!* He was standing in front of a bookshelf all the way in the back, apparently very engrossed in the book he was reading. *Surprise surprise!* I thought, and began wandering over to where he was.

"Looks like you left your dog behind today," I said.

"Yeah," he smiled. "It's this rain. I left him back at the inn."

"How is it that you've got a dog when you don't even have a house?"

"I talked to the people at the inn and they agreed to let me keep him chained up in the back garden. I mean, I've been staying there for a while now and I've gotten to be pretty good friends with them, you know? Sometimes when I have nothing else to do I help them lay out the futons in the bedrooms and stuff. The only problem is that I can't tell them why I'm here. It's kind of a bizarre feeling, almost like I'm a spy or something."

"Yeah, I know what you mean." I nodded. After all, Kyōichi's parents owned that huge hotel that was going up at the base of the mountain, and to a greater or lesser degree all the innkeepers in town had the hotel on their minds. Come to think of it, this summer was probably pretty hard on him, too.

"Where's Tsugumi today?" asked Kyōichi. "She's not with you?"

Maybe it's just hindsight, but I seem to recall that as I heard him say Tsugumi's name, noticing the special clarity and deliberateness with which he pronounced it, my chest flooded for just a moment with an intuition that Tsugumi's love might be headed into a bright future. Focusing my gaze on the transparent beads of rain that kept dripping from the plastic awning at the front of the store, I replied, "Tsugumi's at home, lying in her futon. You wouldn't know it to look at her, but actually she's incredibly frail. Hey listen, Kyōichi . . . if you don't have any plans or anything, you know, why don't you come pay her a visit? I bet she'd like that a lot."

"Yeah, sure, if you think that won't make her feel even worse," he replied. "You know, I guess now that you mention it she is unusually thin and pale, isn't she? She's a pretty interesting girl, isn't she?"

I'm afraid I can't explain this very well. But just then, as the lucid rush of the rain went on closing over the town, little by little, I felt utterly convinced that something about the two of them was right.

I'd been living in Tokyo and going to school there since spring, and I'd had the chance to see an awful lot of couples. (That's kind of a weird way to put it, I guess—makes me sound like I'd never been out of the boonies.) And I have to admit that I could sense what it was that had drawn all those people together. When you spend a lot of time with a couple, even two people who seem totally mismatched at first glance, you usually end up discovering some aspect of their relationship that makes their being together seem perfectly logical. It could be that they resemble one other, or that their lifestyles or their tastes in clothing are simi-

lar—there's always something like that. But what I felt in
Tsugumi and Kyōichi that day, in that sudden instant of understanding, was something much stronger, something incredibly
powerful. *Yes . . . earlier, when Kyōichi said her name, my images of*
the two of them fused, slipped together for just a moment, and the double
image glittered . . . I saw that the concentration of interest each
felt in the other had managed to slice through the dull, rainy
afternoon—that the two of them had made a connection. I had
confidence in this intuition of mine. And I had the impression
that this force I had sensed in them was what people refer to as
fate, the beginning of a fabulous love.

I remained lost in these thoughts as we walked, gazing down
at the rainbow of colors sparkling on the wet steaming asphalt
of the dark gray road.

"Hold on, aren't you supposed to take some sort of gift when
you go to see someone who's sick? What sort of things does
Tsugumi like?"

Kyōichi's question made me burst out laughing.

"I'm sure anything's fine. Earlier she told me that she wanted
apple juice, one of those pricey gourmet melons, and some
sushi."

"Hmm . . . " Kyōichi cocked his head, looking puzzled. "It
doesn't really sound like a very good combination, does it?"

It occurred to me that this must be what people mean when
they say that what goes around comes around, and I kept chuckling for ages.

My heart thumping with the excitement of imagining how
Tsugumi would react—the startled look that would flicker into

her eyes and all the little tricks she would use to try and keep us from noticing it—I quietly slid open the door to her room and yelled in, "Look, Tsugumi, you've got company!"

But Tsugumi wasn't there.

The lights were still on, but the only trace of her left in the bright room was the heavy cover on her futon, which remained slightly raised, just as she must have left it when she slid out. I was dumbfounded. True enough, she was constantly doing incomprehensible things like this, but the girl had a fever of about a hundred and two degrees.

"I don't get it . . . she's not here," I muttered.

"Didn't you say she was super-sick?" Kyōichi replied, drawing his eyebrows tightly together in a frown. It was kind of an odd way to put it.

"Yeah, that's true, but—" I found myself at a loss as to how to continue. Then, "Could you wait here a second? I want to take a look downstairs."

I dashed down to the entryway, crouched in front of the shelf where people left their shoes when they came inside, and began hunting around for Tsugumi's sandals—the beach sandals with the white flowers on top that she always wore. I was just relishing the feeling of relief that came the moment I found them lined up neatly among the crowd of sandals belonging to the guests at the inn, when Aunt Masako came walking down the hall.

"Is there something wrong?" she asked.

"Tsugumi isn't in her room."

"What?" she said, her eyes bulging. "But she's running such a terrible fever today! We just had the doctor come a little while

ago—it's only been a few minutes since he gave her the shot!
Maybe the medicine cured the fever, and so she started feeling
like she was better . . . ?"

"I bet that's it."

"But I've been at the front desk this whole time, and no one
has gone past except for you. She must be inside somewhere . . .
At any rate, we'd better see if we can find her," said my aunt,
looking uneasy.

"What is that girl thinking!" I sighed.

We decided to have Kyōichi go and take a look around the
neighborhood, and Aunt Masako and I walked around the inn,
searching for Tsugumi. We tried the guest house, the little
alcove where the vending machines were, and everywhere else.
We opened the door to Yōko's room. But she wasn't anywhere. No Tsugumi. Time after time we strode up and down
the same dim halls of the small building, past doors that were
all shaped the same, the sighing of the rain numbingly ever
present, and gradually I began to slip into a peculiar mood, a
feeling like I had stumbled into some sort of lonely labyrinth.
Marching along, retracing our footsteps again and again under
the light of the fluorescent bulbs, Aunt Masako and I were
suddenly overcome by a quiet sense of helplessness. But come
to think of it, it was always this way—the feeling that seized
us at times like this wasn't so much anxiety or anger as it was
helplessness. These occasions always forced us to remember
that no matter how clearly we saw the brilliantly burning flame
of life that this sassy young woman harbored, her life was re-

ally playing itself out in a place that was fairly sad, and she could never shake off that sadness.

Just spending too much time on the swings . . .

Just half a day swimming at the beach . . .

Just being tired from having gotten caught up in a late-night movie . . .

Just going out without a jacket when there was a slight chill in the air . . .

would make Tsugumi collapse. She would lose strength. The only reason her existence here seemed so unshakably settled was that deep inside her she had a hidden store of energy that rebelled against the frailty of her flesh, struggled ferociously against it . . .

Yes, yes—on rainy days like this my head feels like it's stuffed with cotton, and memories of days long gone come drifting up through my body, marvelously real. I seem to see the color that tinted the air in those days reflected in the dark windowpanes, and it's a tint like the rush of sentiment. The weight of the closed doors in my childish eyes. My mother's voice—"You've got to be quiet, Maria. Tsugumi's condition is very precarious right now." Yōko's eyes filling with tears, her long braids. It happened all the time when I was a child, all the time.

"She just isn't anywhere, is she?"

Arriving at the door to Tsugumi's bedroom, we sighed once more.

Kyōichi called up to us as he climbed the stairs, "She isn't anywhere in this neighborhood." Apparently he hadn't taken an umbrella when he went out, because his hair was drenched.

"Oh dear, look how wet you are! I'm so sorry to have put you to so much trouble," murmured Aunt Masako, sounding very abashed, even though she still had no idea who he was. The order of things was all messed up.

"Do you think that means she's gone somewhere far away?" I asked. And then for some reason or other I headed over toward the veranda, thinking that I might as well take a look outside. I peered out the big window with the wooden frame that opened out over the platform.

And I had found her.

"Here she is . . ." I said weakly, addressing Aunt Masako, and pushed the wobbly window open. It's hard to believe, but Tsugumi had actually crawled down into the opening between the floor of the veranda and the roof that lay below it— the roof of the second story. She peeked up at me through the gap between two boards and, still squatting there, yelled up to me.

"So you figured it out!"

"Figured what out? What on earth are you doing there, Tsugumi?" I said, feeling stunned to the very core of my being. I just didn't get it at all.

"Oh my God, Tsugumi! You went out there barefoot! It must be so cold out there, and you've got nothing on . . . ! Hurry up and get in here! You'll end up with a fever again!" cried my aunt, an expression on her face that made it perfectly clear how relieved she was. She reached out and tugged a very wet Tsugumi out from under the veranda, inching her out a bit at a time. "I'm going to run and get a towel now, so I want you to climb right into your futon and stay there, you hear me?" Aunt Masako bustled off downstairs.

Then I spoke up again. "Tsugumi, what were you doing out

there? Isn't that kind of a strange place for you to be spending your time?"

It's true that in the days when we played hide-and-seek, the space under the veranda had been one of her best hiding places. But then it goes without saying that this was hardly the sort of time to be playing hide-and-seek.

"Gimme a break, kid!" said Tsugumi, shaking into a fit of feverishly giddy laughter. "I saw you out the window! You bring Kyōichi back thinking that you're gonna startle me out of my wits, and you're prancing along with this gleeful look on your face, totally full of yourself . . . figured I might as well give you a taste of your own medicine . . ."

"Your mother sure is nice, isn't she?" said Kyoichi. At first he had been worrying that his presence might make things awkward, and he had said that it might be best for him to leave, but my aunt and Tsugumi and I all struggled mightily to convince him not to go, and eventually he'd agreed to remain and have a cup of tea. "I mean, she didn't yell at you at all."

"Her love for her daughter is deeper than the sea," said Tsugumi.

Liar, I thought. The only reason Aunt Masako remained so unperturbed was that she'd grown accustomed to having Tsugumi put her through all sorts of misery like this. I figured Kyōichi was bound to reach this conclusion on his own sooner or later, though, so I just kept sipping my tea in silence. I had also noticed that every time Kyōichi turned to looked at Tsugumi, his gaze was overflowing with sympathy, as if he were eyeing a kitten headed for the grave, and I didn't want to rain on his parade. And though in a certain sense I was feeling just as cool and collected as my tone here suggests, Tsugumi appeared to be in such pain that even I got a bit concerned about her condition. There were dark circles under her eyes, her breath came quickly, and her lips were as white as they could be. Thin strands of drenched hair clung to her forehead, and her eyes and cheeks were so shiny they seemed to gleam.

Kyōichi stood up. "Well, I think I'll head back now. Catch you two later. Quit playing these infantile games and stay in bed like you ought to, Tsugumi. You gotta hurry up and get well, hear me?"

"Hold on a second!" Tsugumi cried. She grabbed my arm with a hand so hot it was frightening. "Maria, don't just let the scoundrel leave! Stop him!" she shouted, her voice hoarse.

I looked up at Kyōichi. "Sounds like she wants you to stay," I said. "Could you stick around a little longer?"

"What is it?" Kyōichi said, coming back over near her pillow.

"Won't you tell me a story?" Tsugumi pleaded. "Ever since I was a little girl I've never been able to fall asleep unless someone tells me a new story."

Liar, I thought once more. But at the same time I was really impressed by the words "a new story." They sounded sweet, had a nice kind of tang.

"Let's see . . . a story. All right then, if it will help you settle down and go to sleep, I'll tell you 'The Story of the Towel,'" said Kyōichi.

"The towel?" I said. Tsugumi looked as nonplussed as I was.

"When I was a kid," Kyōichi continued, "I had this problem with my heart. So we were waiting until I got a little older, you know, until my body became strong enough that they could operate. Of course this is all old news, I've had the operation now and I'm as healthy as I can be, and I hardly ever think of those days. But when something really awful happens, when I run into some kind of trouble, when I'm really hurting bad, I always remember the towel . . . Back in those days I was completely bedridden; I was a kid who never got up. There was no guarantee that the operation would even help, but still I had to keep on waiting. Most of the time it was okay waiting for something like that, for something that couldn't even be counted on to help, but whenever I had an attack . . . man, let me tell you, I got so depressed and worried that it couldn't have been any worse. It was such torture I didn't know what to do."

The sighing of the rain seemed to fade. We both concentrated intently on the utterly unexpected story Kyōichi was telling. He was speaking casually but very clearly. His voice filled the quiet room.

"Every time I had an attack I would force myself to lie there and not think of anything. If I closed my eyes my mind would start going through all kinds of stuff that I really didn't want to think about, and I hated being in the dark, so I'd keep my eyes open the whole time. I would just lie there waiting for the pain to pass. You know how people say that if you meet up with a bear you should lie there acting like you're dead? Well I think I can understand how people in that situation feel, because it's probably the same way I felt then. It was awful, really awful. So anyway, I had this one-of-a-kind pillowcase that was made out of this fancy towel that my grandmother gave my mother when she got married to my father. The towel had been made overseas somewhere. It was very important to my mother and she'd used it for ages, and then when the edges started coming unraveled she sewed it into a pillowcase for me. It had a really cool design—all these multicolored flags from foreign countries lined up against a deep blue background. The mix of colors was very sharp, lots of contrast, and I would just keep staring at it and staring at it as I lay there, from that lying-down angle. That's how I would pass my time . . . At the time I didn't really think much about it, but later on—right before I had the operation, for example, and after the operation, when things were really hard, and even now, every time I run into some kind of problem—at times like that the design of that towel always catapults into my mind. The thing has been gone for ages and ages, but I see it so clearly it actually seems to be there in front of me, right in front of my eyes. It's as if I could just reach out and grab it. And it's strange—as soon as I see that design I start feeling like I'm in control again. I've decided that I should think of it as a kind of faith. Pretty interesting story in its way, don't you think? The end."

"Wow . . ." I said.

His unruffled calm, the maturity you sensed in his behavior, the aura of properness about him that was like a neatly drawn line, and especially those eyes—no doubt living through such a childhood was what had made him turn out this way. And though the way in which Tsugumi reflected her experience was the exact opposite of this, she too had walked a similar, solitary path. Yes, it was a work of nature, and there wasn't anything that could be done about it, but still it hurt to think of Tsugumi's heart beating away in that broken body. Her spirit had strength like the raging of a fire that could reach out into the depths of space, burning deeper than anyone's, but her body kept it locked in extreme confinement. Maybe this pointless energy of hers had led her to sense, at a glance, what it was that shone in Kyōichi's eyes?

Tsugumi looked at Kyōichi. "You'd gaze at those flags and think about all those faraway countries? And about the place you would go after you died?" she asked. It was the kind of question that makes your heart leap.

"All the time," said Kyōichi.

"And now you've managed to change yourself into the kind of person who can go anywhere. Man, I wish I were like that," Tsugumi said.

"Yeah, you've gotta be like that, too . . . No, I take that back," Kyōichi said quietly. "Being able to go anywhere isn't the point. Hey, it's nice here, too. You can wander around in your sandals, wander around in your bathing suit, and you've got the mountains and the ocean. You've got a sturdy spirit and you've got guts—even if you were to end up spending your entire life here you'd get to see more than all these bozos who make trips around the world. That's the sort of feeling I get from you."

"Be nice if that were true." Tsugumi smiled. There was a sparkle in her eyes, and her cheeks were flushed. She parted her lips slightly in a quick grin, displaying her white teeth. It seemed her white comforter might catch the faintly glossy red of her cheeks, toss back the faintest of reflections. That day it didn't take much to make me cry, and now I found myself looking down, blinking. Just then Tsugumi turned her gaze directly on Kyōichi.

"I'm in love with you, babe," she said.

Swimming with My Father

The sight of Tsugumi wandering along the beach with Kyōichi—this new amour of hers—created something of a stir in town. They stood out so much it was weird, it really was. You wouldn't think we'd see anything odd in this combination of "Tsugumi + Male," since we had been accustomed to seeing it for a very long time already, but somehow Tsugumi and Kyōichi always had this aura about them as they walked around our small town—like sweethearts rambling aimlessly through some distant land, they seemed to give off a halo of delicate, uncertain light. They were always on the beach, and they always had the dogs with them. The faraway sparkle in their eyes seemed like it must make everyone who glimpsed it think back on something precious, call up the pleasant ache of a reviving memory, like a dream dreamt long ago.

Back at home she still tormented her family, kicked Pooch's food around, refused to apologize, and turned up stretched out here or there or somewhere else with her stomach showing, snoring her nose off. When she was with Kyōichi, on the other hand, she shone with a look of such utter happiness that you got the feeling she must have sped up the pace of her life somehow,

that she was fighting to cram more life into each passing moment. Looking at her you felt a touch of unease—a feeling that
seemed to flicker painfully through the depths of your chest, the
way light glimmers through a hole in a cloud.

Tsugumi's style of living always called up this fear.

Her emotions seemed to yank her body this way and that; they
appeared to be whittling away at her life so quickly it was dizzy-
ing; they were dazzling.

"Hey, Mar-i-a-a!" My father stuck his hand out the window of the
bus and waved to me, hollering in a voice so loud that I could only
sit there stunned, my mouth agape, blushing. I stood up and went
over to the bus stop. My eyes were trained on the giant bus as it
slowly turned in from the highway and headed toward me, groaning loudly and sending out ripples of heat. The summer light made
the scene look very solemn. And then the door opened and my
father emerged in a stream of colorful tourists.

My mother hadn't come. She'd said on the phone that going
to the shore and seeing the same summer ocean as always would
make her feel so nostalgic and sad that she was bound to start
crying, and that was something she'd rather not have to go
through. I figured she was planning to slip down very quietly at
the beginning of autumn and see the Yamamoto Inn through its
final days, when the preparations for moving got under way.
Anyway, my dad absolutely refused to give up, saying that he
would go alone if he had to. His head filled with dreams of A
Vacation with My Grown-up Daughter, he had come to spend
the night. I found it kind of funny how everything had changed
so much. After all, it wasn't that long ago that he'd been com-

ing on the weekends to visit my mother and me. Yes . . . every summer since I was a child I'd relished the pleasure of sitting on the thoroughly baked concrete steps in my hat and my sandals, feeling the hot sun beating down on my skin as I waited for my father's bus to arrive. He always came on the bus because boats made him seasick. So I would sit there patiently, looking forward to the soft scene that would play itself out between us, the reunion of a daughter and a father who lived apart. Most of the time my mother couldn't get away from the inn, so I'd make my way to the bus stop through the daytime sun all alone. I'd scan the windows of each giant bus as it arrived, searching for my father's face.

I went through the same routine in autumn and winter and spring, but for some reason when I think back on those days now it seems as if it was always summer. When my father stepped down from the bus his face would shine with a powerful smile, as if he had been holding in something unbearable, and the sunlight was always so bright you could hardly stand to look.

My father had put on sunglasses in an attempt to make himself look young, and seeing him like that gave me a shock, sent me reeling from my childhood back into my nineteen-year-old self. I stood up. It was so sweltering out that we seemed to have landed in some sort of dream, a world where everything was dizzily whirling. I felt unable to speak.

"Ah, smell that sea breeze!" sighed my father, the hair on his forehead swishing around lightly in the wind.

"Welcome back!" I said.

"Turned into a local again, I see. Got a tan and everything!"

"How's Mom?"

"She decided to stay away, just like she said, so she's just relaxing at home. Said to give you her love."

"Yeah, I figured she wouldn't come. Aunt Masako said she didn't expect her either. God, it's been a while since I came to meet you here, hasn't it?"

"It sure has," said my father quietly, as if to himself.

"What do you want to do? Should we go drop off your luggage first? You can say hello to Aunt Masako and everyone, and then . . . what do you feel like doing? You want to take the car and drive somewhere?"

"Nope, I'm going swimming!" said my father. His voice sounded very sharp and excited, as if he had been waiting to say this for a long time. "More than anything else, I came here to swim."

My father didn't used to swim.

It was as if he refused to let The Ocean enter at all into the time he spent together with my mother and me, our time as a family. As if he were afraid that the small periods of relaxation we shared would get lost in the languid, light-filled bustle of the midsummer beach. My mother was my father's lover, the mistress of a married man, but she wasn't at all afraid of being in the public eye, and so in the evenings when her work in the kitchen came to a temporary halt she would fix up her hair and change her clothes and come get me, and then she and my father and I would set out on a cheerful walk. The time we spent walking together like this—two parents and their daughter strolling along a shore that seemed to rise to meet the twilight—those moments were the happiest we knew. Silhouettes of dragonflies would dance against a deep purple-blue sky while I licked away at the Popsicle they had bought me. Usually the wind had died down by then, and the hot air that lingered on the beach hung close around us, smelling of the tide. The Popsicle always tasted too weak to hold on to—as if the flavor was already spiraling away into the past. My mother's face looked white and blurry, and in the light of the few trails of clouds that still glimmered way off in the west I found her extremely beautiful, found the line of her profile soft and gentle. When my father walked alongside my mother, the shoulders that moved in line with hers seemed so solidly real that I found it hard to believe he had only just arrived from Tokyo.

The sand settled into patterns like waves in the tracks of the wind, and the only sound that echoed across the empty beach was the almost too loud pounding of the waves.

You feel really lonely when someone keeps coming and going all the time. And I had a hunch that somehow the loneliness I suffered in my father's absence contained a vague shadow of death.

My father was always there on the weekends, but when I awoke on Monday mornings he'd be gone, leaving no trace that he'd even been there at all. And as young as I was, the thought of leaving my futon then really frightened me. I'd do what I could to put off asking my mother if he'd gone, having my father's absence become a positive fact. But just as I began slipping back into a terrible, halfhearted, lonely sleep, my mother would strip off my covers.

"Rise and shine! You'll be late for your exercises!" she'd say, smiling.

The dazzling brilliance of that smile called up our ordinary lives, the days we passed without my father. A feeling of relief would surge over me.

"Is Dad gone?" I'd ask in a voice fuzzy with sleep, just to make sure.

My mother would smile a little sadly before she answered. "He left for Tokyo on the first bus this morning."

I'd lie there for a while gazing through the screen at the morning outside, my eyes still sleepy, thinking about my father. How I went to meet his bus . . . the artless smile on his face as he wrapped his big hand around mine, making no move to let go even when I told him it was too hot to hold hands . . . the three of us walking together in the evening.

Yōko would always come to get me right around then, and we would stride out into the still-cool morning and head for the park, on our way to join the other kids in town in the daily exercise program run by the radio station.

As I watched my father gradually vanish into the distant waves, I found myself suddenly recalling the mood of those mornings. The feeling was so clear it was like experiencing it all over again.

As soon as we'd arrived at the beach and he'd changed into his swimsuit, my unable-to-wait-a-second-longer father yelled that he was going in ahead of me and dashed off toward the edge of the water. I noticed that starting from his elbows, his arms and hands were shaped just like mine—the resemblance was so striking that it gave me kind of a shock. *No mistaking it,* I thought, as I continued smearing myself with sunscreen, *that man really is my father.*

The sun was high and brilliant, beating down with such ferocity that it bleached everything on the shore, turning it all

vividly white. The sea was so calm you would almost think it
was a lake, hardly a wave out there. Raising his voice in childish
shrieks, yelling, *It's so cold! Man, is it cold!* my father slowly disappeared into the water. He was heading out beyond the break-
ers. You got the impression that he was being dragged out by
the water, rather than moving of his own accord. The expanse
of blue was so infinitely vast that the scenery had no problem at
all absorbing a person or two. I got up and sprinted into the
ocean, chasing my father. I'm in love with the moment when
the water switches from being so cold you want to leap up into
the air to something that feels just right against your skin. Looking up, I saw the mountains that encircle the sea flashing their
shimmering green out over the water, soaring up against a blue
background of sky. All this greenery so close to the shore looked
unbelievably thick and clear.

My father had already swum out pretty far. He still had a long
way to go before you could call him elderly, but he was also more
than old enough to be supporting a family for the first time in his
life. He really wasn't that far off, only a few yards ahead, and yet
as he swam his head kept appearing framed in the dizzyingly bright
valley of the long, shining ocean, only to disappear again into the
tight blue commotion of the waves—his head seemed so terribly
tiny, so close to vanishing . . . this was what had made me think
about his age. As I swam on, a vague feeling of unease began to
take hold of me. Maybe it was because the water was cold, or
maybe it was because for a while now I had been swimming in
water so deep that my feet couldn't touch the bottom. Or perhaps it was the strength of the sun, or the way the clouds changed
shape every time I blinked—perhaps that was what opened the

way for these thoughts to sneak into me, I don't know. *I'm losing sight of my father . . . we're going to end up lost on the far side of these waves . . . never to return, vanished . . .* No, that isn't it. It's nothing as physical as that. It's just that I don't really have a good grasp on our life in Tokyo yet. Here in this ocean, in the midst of all this water, with the red flags on those distant buoys flapping in the sea breeze, I find myself unable to treat our house in Tokyo as anything but a dream. I saw my father swimming in front of me, his hands cutting through the water, but that was simply part of another faraway dream. Maybe deep down I still hadn't managed to work through it all—maybe in the end I was still exactly what I'd been back then, a little girl who waited all alone for her father to arrive, weekend after weekend . . .

Back then, when things at work got too busy and my father showed up with a totally worn-out expression on his face, there was something my mother would say to him. She wasn't trying to be unpleasant, and it wasn't like she was really worried, because she would always say it with a smile.

"You know, if something ever happened to you, Maria and I aren't in the kind of position where we'd be able to rush up to Tokyo to see you, and we certainly wouldn't be able to come to your funeral. I don't want that to happen, so you've really got to take better care of your health. Understand?"

I was only a child, but even so I understood. Yes, in the uncertainty of our days my father always seemed like he was about to depart for someplace very far away, never to return. That's the kind of man he was for me.

These memories were still crowding my mind when my father turned his head to look at me, squinting his eyes in the sunlight. He stopped swimming. Stroke by stroke I closed in on him, plowing across the valleys between waves. As the distance between us dwindled, my father smiled.

"I decided I'd better let you catch up," he said.

Light exploded on the water into millions of individual flecks, an array so dazzling that it made me catch my breath. As my father and I swam together toward a nearby buoy, my thoughts continued to race.

When Dad catches the bullet train back to Tokyo tomorrow, I just know he's going to have about a ton of packages of dried fish and conches and all kinds of other stuff, and he'll hardly be able to carry it all. My mother will be standing in the kitchen, and she'll turn around to look at him and ask how I'm doing and how everyone else is doing . . . The scene rose up before me, almost transparent, like a vision, making me so happy I started to feel a bit dizzy. *I'm happy to be what I am, a single daughter in this family.* Yes, it was true. This seaside town where I'd grown up was no longer mine, but I had somewhere else to return to, an unshakably real home of my own.

I had come out of the water and was lazing about on the beach when I felt the bottom of someone's bare foot slam down onto the palm of my hand and start squashing it. When I opened my eyes Tsugumi was peering down at me. With all the light streaming around from behind, her white skin and her large, intensely glittering eyes were so bright it was hard to look.

"God, Tsugumi, was it really necessary for you to stomp on my hand like that?" I moaned. "I mean, no warning or anything!" Figuring I had no choice, I sat up.

"Listen, kid, just be glad I didn't do it with my sandal on."

Tsugumi finally removed her faintly warm foot from my palm and put her sandal back on. My father sat up next to me with a groan.

"Hey there, Tsugumi!" he said.

"Howdy, Uncle. Long time no see."

Tsugumi had squatted down beside me. She looked over at my father and grinned. A long time had passed since we stopped attending the same school, and seeing her smile in this meant-for-the-public way made me feel strangely nostalgic, calling up memories of her as a school-uniformed child. Playing angel at school was one of her favorite pastimes. For a moment I wondered if Kyōichi would ever have managed to discover her if they had gone to the same school, but I decided very quickly that he would have. Kyōichi had the same sort of unbalanced view of the world as Tsugumi, where you focus your entire life on a single thing and just keep digging down deeper and deeper into it. People like the two of them would be able to find each other blindfolded.

"So what's up, Tsugumi? Where are you headed?" I asked.

There was a strong wind blowing, and I could feel sand swishing about in tiny swirls around my feet, then whirling off.

"Got a date. Pretty swell, huh?" Tsugumi said, giving me such a dazzling smile you had the impression it might spill over the top of her face. "I'm not one of these losers you come across on the beach spending their time dozing with their daddies, if you catch my drift."

I let this pass just as I always do, but since my father hadn't been properly Tsugumi-ized like the rest of us, his face took on a sort of puzzled expression.

"Well you know, when you've spent as much time living apart as we have, a grown daughter does come to seem somewhat like a lover," he said. "Listen, Tsugumi, if you have the time, why not sit down with us and enjoy the sea."

"I see your old man is still cracking his vulgar jokes," said Tsugumi. "But I suppose it wouldn't hurt to sit down for a while before I go. To tell the truth, in my eagerness to get the guy I left the house a little early."

Tsugumi plopped down on our plastic spread. She gazed out at the ocean, squinting against the light. Just beyond her, the curve of our beach umbrella cut sharply into the blue sky, flapping crazily, noisily in the wind. It was such an amazingly bright, vivid scene that I lay there unable to tear my gaze away. My heart felt as if it might flutter off to some place far away.

"It sounds like you're in love, Tsugumi," said my father. He's a nice guy, he really is. In the past his niceness had created all sorts of barriers, keeping life from progressing as he wished, but now that things had ended up peacefully he seemed calm and bright, like those lines of mountains shining in the sun. Now, watching his goodness work its magic in a world where everything had settled into place, the change seemed truly sacred and good.

"Boy oh boy, am I ever!" Tsugumi cried, then flopped down alongside me, plopping her head down on the bag I'd brought with me as if she had every right in the world to do so.

"You'll run a fever if you get sunburned," I said.

"Women in love are strong." Tsugumi laughed.

Without a word I picked up my hat and lay it over her face.

"Yeah, you're right—the only reason I've managed to live this long, and the reason my skin is so fair, and the reason I'm able to relish my food as much as I do is that Maria here fusses over me so!" she warbled, and put on the hat.

"You seem to have grown a lot stronger, Tsugumi," said my father.

"How lovely of you to notice," said Tsugumi.

All three of us were now lying in a line, gazing up at the sky, which seemed kind of strange for some reason. Every so often a cloud would float by slowly overhead, the sky beyond it shining faintly through.

"Are you really that deeply in love with him?"

"Not as much as you're in love, I'll grant you that. Hell, all the years you spent as a commuting husband! I was wondering how things would turn out, and damn it if you didn't push that love right through to the end!"

Tsugumi and my father got along really well. Tsugumi's own father was a very inflexible, almost overly masculine, type of person—lots of times he would get angry over one of Tsugumi's cheeky remarks and suddenly leap up and stalk away from the dinner table without even saying a word. Of course Tsugumi has never been the slightest bit bothered by things like that; she just goes right on living her own life. But my father isn't simply a wishy-washy fellow who finds it hard to take a stance; he also recognizes the difference between good and bad intentions. He sees that Tsugumi doesn't have any real malice in her. Their conversation now was so adorable that I felt a kind of tender-ness welling up inside me as I listened.

"I'm the sort of person who can never give up on anything until it's really finished, I'll admit that, but I get the feeling that in this case it may have had more to do with the qualities of the partner I've found," my father said.

"Yeah, she seems pretty tenacious, doesn't she? And of course there's no denying that she's one hell of a looker. I was betting that she'd end up staying here her whole life, and that you'd keep doing the commuting husband thing right up to the end. After all, that's the true path of the righteous lover, huh?"

"That might have been possible, as long as an end was in sight," replied my father earnestly. Looking at him you would have thought he was talking to the goddess of destiny, rather than to some young girl. "Love is the kind of thing that's already happening by the time you notice it, that's how it works, and no matter how old you get, that doesn't change. Except that you can break it up into two entirely distinct types—love where there's an end in sight and love where there isn't. People in love understand that better than anyone. When there's no end in sight, it means you're headed for something huge. After I first got to know Maria's mom, the future started to feel totally unlimited, all of a sudden. So yeah, I guess you could say that maybe we didn't even need to get married."

"Then what would have become of me?" I said, just as a joke.

"Yeah, we had you, and now we're happy, right?" My father stretched his arms up like a boy, looking out over the ocean and the mountains and the sky. "I certainly don't have any complaints. This is the greatest!"

"You know, the way you're so simple that you just come out and say things like that—I kinda like it. You're one of the few guys around who's able to put me in such an obliging mood," said Tsugumi, her face very serious.

My father chuckled, looking pleased. "Is that right? Seems like you must have been pretty popular with the guys all along. Do you like this guy more than you liked any of the others?" he asked.

Tsugumi cocked her head slightly and replied in a whisper, almost as if she were talking to herself. "Hard to say . . . It kinda seems like something I've been through before, but on the other hand I guess you could say that it was never really like this. I mean, until now, no matter what happened, even if the guy were to break down and start bawling right in front of me, no matter how much I liked him, he could start bugging me to let him hold my hand or touch me or whatever, but somehow . . . I don't know . . . it just always seemed like I was stuck at the edge. I was on the shore of this river, in the dark, looking at this fire burning on the other side. I could see just how long it would take for the fire to burn down, you know, and it was so boring I thought I might fall asleep. Because all that stuff always ends right on time, you know? I really couldn't see what those guys were looking for in love, at our age."

"I agree with you there. Sooner or later people are definitely going to give up if you don't give them back as much as they're giving you," my father said.

"But you know, this time I really feel like I'm participating. Perhaps it's because of the dogs, or because I'll be moving. But Kyōichi is different. No matter how many times we get together I never get sick of being with him, and every time I look into his eyes I just want to take the ice cream or whatever I've got in my hand and rub it into his face. That's how much I like him."

"I don't think Kyōichi would really go for that," I said. But even as I spoke I felt her words sinking into me, sinking me deep in thought. Hot sand brushed against the soles of my feet, silky smooth. Somehow the sensation made me want to start praying. *Please let Tsugumi be visited by nothing but good from now on—* over and over, in time with the roaring of the waves.

"I see," said my father. "Introduce me to this guy sometime."
Tsugumi nodded and said she would.

The next day I went to see my father off. He was taking a bus
headed directly for Tokyo, an express. He was heading home.

"Say hi to Mom for me," I said.

My newly tanned father nodded. Just as I'd expected, he was
taking back such a load of various seafoods that he couldn't carry
it all, even using both hands. He had so much stuff you wondered just who he expected to eat it all. I figured my mother
would end up being put to lots of trouble, going around distrib-
uting stuff to the neighbors. It was a scene I knew, one that had
sent its roots deep down into me by now, and I could see it
clearly. Like the lines of buildings in Tokyo, and the strangely
subdued dinners the three of us ate together. Like the sound of
my returning father's footsteps.

The bus stop was flooded with late afternoon light, and the
reflected orange glow was bright enough to make me squint.
The bus drew in just as slowly as the one my father had come
on, and my father got on; then the bus pulled out into the street,
still moving slowly. My father never stopped waving.

I felt a little lonely as I strolled back to the inn through the gathering dusk, alone this time. I wanted to hold on to the particular
feeling of languor that I got as I walked the streets of this town,
the town of my past, which I would lose when summer ended.
This world of ours is piled high with farewells and goodbyes of so
many different kinds, like the evening sky renewing itself again
and again from one instant to the next—and I didn't want to forget a single one.

Festival

Not long after the number of vacationers hits its peak and starts declining, this town holds its summer festival. Which is to say that it's an event staged in large part for the locals. The activities are centered around this big Shinto shrine up on one of the mountains. Crowds of stalls are set up in two long rows along the spacious cobblestone walkway that cuts through the middle of the shrine, and a stage is assembled for people to perform regional variations of two ancient festival rites, the *o-bon* and *kagura* dances. Out on the beach there's an enormous display of fireworks.

Right around the time when the hustle and bustle of preparations for the festival take ahold of the town, all of a sudden you find yourself noticing that autumn has begun weaving itself into the rhythm of your days. The sun is still just as strong as before, but the breeze blowing in off the sea has turned just the tiniest bit softer, and the sand has cooled. Now the rain that quietly drenches the boats ranged along the beach carries the damp, misty smell of a cloudy sky. You realize that summer has turned its back on you.

*　*　*

One day shortly before the festival, I came down with a fever and had to take to my futon—perhaps because I'd let myself get swept up in all the excitement and worn myself out having a good time. Tsugumi happened to be laid up too, so Yōko ended up shuttling back and forth between our two rooms like a nurse, bringing us ice packs and bowls of creamed rice that were supposed to help us get well. She kept telling us over and over that we had to hurry and get better before the festival.

It's extremely rare for me to come down with a fever, so just thinking that my temperature had inched up over one hundred degrees was enough to make my head start spinning. With things as they were, there really was nothing I could do but lie there in my futon, my face glowing red.

A little before dusk Tsugumi shoved open the sliding door and sauntered into my room, following her usual policy of giving me absolutely no warning at all before she entered. I had been lying completely motionless, gazing out the window into a ruby red sky that extended so far into the distance it was scary. My whole body felt heavy and dull and I really didn't want to have to bother with Tsugumi, so I just lay as I was, keeping my gaze directed out the window, not even turning to look at her.

"So babe, *you* got a fever, huh?" Tsugumi growled, kicking me in the back. Figuring that if she was going to be like this I didn't have much of a choice, I rolled over and swiveled my head around to face her. She had her hair pulled back and tied up in a single knot, and was wearing a pair of cheerful light blue pajamas. She looked as if she were feeling fine.

"Look who's talking! You sure don't look so feverish to me," I said.

"Listen missy, this much is normal for me." Tsugumi grinned. My hand had been lying outside the covers, so she picked it up and squeezed it in hers. "Yeah, I'd say we're running just about the same temperature."

It was true. Usually when Tsugumi had a fever her hands were so hot that it blew my mind, but now they didn't even feel particularly warm.

"I guess you're really used to being sick, aren't you?" I said.

The realization that Tsugumi was constantly running around in a state like the one I was in now hit me with a new strength, and I felt a swell of emotion. Feverish eyes see a world in limbo, one that soars up aggressively. Your heart flaps around with a lightness that balances the heaviness of your body, and your thoughts keep getting tangled up again and again in unfamiliar ideas.

Tsugumi squatted down beside my pillow.

"Yeah, I guess you could say that," she said. "But then my body's so weak that I get totally pooped in next to no time. It sucks, it really does."

"Luckily mademoiselle's spirit has enough kick for two," I grinned.

"If only one could live on spirit alone," said Tsugumi, grinning back.

All summer long, Tsugumi was just as lovely as she could be. Something inside her kept creating an endless number of these moments—scenes when the whole world would have caught its breath at the sight of her, and stood staring, utterly enchanted. The contented smile that lit up her face seemed as pure and rare as the final flurry of spring snow on a mountaintop.

"You know how everything looks really weird when you've

got a fever? Don't you think it's kind of fun?" Tsugumi narrowed her eyes a little as she spoke. There was something strangely gentle in her expression. She seemed like some tiny creature delighted to have found itself a partner.

"Things do seem kind of new," I said.

"Chicks like me who are always getting sick—we just keep commuting back and forth between this and the normal state, right? Eventually you stop being able to tell which one is the real world, and your life rockets by really fast. Everything moves at this totally awesome speed."

"Like always being drunk or something."

"Bingo, babe. Exactly."

Tsugumi gave me a grin, then stood up and left the room. Her departure was just as sudden as her arrival. For a long time the curve of her back lingered in my mind's eye like some sort of afterimage, incredibly clear.

Tsugumi and I were both completely recovered by the night of the festival. We made plans to go out as a party of four— Tsugumi, Kyōichi, Yōko, and me. The prospect of showing her guy what summer festivals in this town were all about had Tsugumi just about as wired as she could be.

For the first time in a year, Tsugumi, Yōko, and I helped each other put on the light cotton kimonos that we always wore to this festival. Each of us could wrap an obi around the waist of the other two, and we all knew how to tie the special knot at the back, but it was impossible for us to get the lengthy pieces of cloth wound around our own waists. Our kimonos were all a dim navy blue, a shade that set off the large white floral pattern, making the flowers glow. We unfolded the blue, spread it out across the spacious tatami-matted floor in one of the rooms of the inn, then laid out the various flashy, stunningly cheap-looking obi, which were all either pink or red. Tsugumi slipped into her kimono, and I picked up a red obi, wrapped it around her waist, and tied it. At times like this, I realize how thin she really is. It feels as if no matter how hard I pull, there will always be a little crevice of darkness beyond . . . I get the feeling that in a moment I'll find myself standing here with nothing left in my hand but the thin, shiff obi . . . A shiver runs along my spine.

We were down in the lobby in our kimonos, watching TV, when Kyōichi came to get us. He had on the same sort of clothes he always wore, but when Tsugumi accused him of being "one hell of a wet blanket" he stuck out one of his feet, pointing out that the footwear was special. He had on a pair of tall wooden clogs of the sort people in Japan used to wear. His large bare feet were like an emblem of summer. And unlike all the other times when I've seen her dressed in a kimono, Tsugumi refrained from bragging about how magnificent she looked. Instead, she stretched out her pale arms and took Kyōichi's hand in hers, yanking it up and down.

"Come on, hurry up, let's go already!" she urged, sounding just like a child. "We want to see all the stalls before the fireworks start!"

Something about the way she said this made it sound extremely adorable.

Then, "Oh my gosh! What happened to you, Kyōichi?"

Until Yōko said this, neither Tsugumi nor I had noticed. He was standing in a slightly shadowy part of the entryway, and it was already starting to fade, but now that we were paying attention we could see that he had a deep blue bruise under one of his eyes.

"Don't tell me—I bet my old man figured out we're dating and socked you one, didn't he? Oh man, that really sucks!" said Tsugumi.

"Yeah, you're telling me." Kyōichi smiled ruefully.

"Oh my God, are you serious?" I cried.

"Hell no, I don't have any idea what happened! Besides, use your brain. You think the old man loves me that much?" Tsugumi was snickering, but her words had a painfully lonely ring. In the end this comment distracted us, and we left the house without having managed to find out what had happened.

Gazing up at the Milky Way where it shone mistily in the sky, we strolled to the end of the street and passed the beach. The music for the *o-bon* dance that streamed from the speakers up at the shrine was buoyed along on the wind, so that you could hear it all over town. The sea looked much blacker and choppier than usual—perhaps because of the way the beach glowed in the light of the lanterns that lined it. People walked more slowly than usual, unwilling to see the summer go. Every little alleyway was crowded with people; it seemed like everyone in town must be out in the streets.

We ran into lots of old friends.

Friends from elementary school, junior high, high school. Everyone had matured in their own way, and even as we stood face to face with them they seemed like people from dreams, sudden glimpses through the fences of our tangled memories. We smiled and waved, exchanged a few words, and then walked on in our separate directions. The singing of flutes, the waving fans, the passing breath of a salty breeze—all this projected itself slowly onto the night, flowing on and on like paper lanterns adrift on a river.

It's impossible to remember the air of a festival night—you have to wait until a festival actually rolls around to get it back. Maybe you're only missing one tiny little detail, but that's all it takes to keep you from reliving the perfect image, calling up the sense of being there. *Will I return to this town again next year? Or will I be missing all this somewhere under that Tokyo sky, caught in my own dream of an imperfect festival?* For a while as we looked up and down the long lines of illuminated stalls I let myself dwell on these thoughts.

The incident occurred while we were standing in the long line of people waiting to pray at the main shrine. Not that it was really much of an incident.

Tsugumi decided it was too much of a pain to wait in line and tried to lead us past without even stopping, and Yōko and I had to fight hard to persuade her that this was the one part of the festival you simply couldn't skip.

Seeing that she had no choice, she lined up beside us.

Even then she wouldn't stop muttering, and kept firing all kinds of saucy comments at us. "Come on kids, you really believe in these 'god' things? No joke? At your age?" she scoffed. "You go up there and chuck the coin in the box and clap three times and you think something good is gonna happen? You really believe that, huh?"

At times like this Kyōichi always kept quiet, his mouth bent in a tiny smile. The particular way he had of keeping quiet struck you as being totally natural, though, and somehow his silence radiated a really awesome sense of presence. Seeing him like this you got a splendid sense of just how selfish and egocentric Tsugumi could act in front of him without it bothering him in the least. Tsugumi has always been good at getting people like him on her side. Maybe because she really needs them.

Whatever else you might say about the shrine, it was certainly just about as crowded as it could be, and the line of people waiting to pray stretched all the way back to the steps leading up to the front gateway. The clunking of the hanging rattle that people shook before praying and the clink of coins falling into the wooden collection box continued without pause while the line slowly pushed forward. Step by step we advanced toward the shrine, chatting about this and that as we waited. Occasionally people cut between us, breaking through the line to get to the other side. Everyone was squashed up against everyone else, so this was only natural. But then suddenly this guy forced himself into the space between Kyōichi and Tsugumi, and stomped through, shoving them both roughly aside. The guy was scrawny and young, a perfect example of the type people refer to as "little punks" and "hoodlums," and he was followed by two or three of his companions, guys more or less like him.

Of course there's no denying that their manner of getting through the line could have been a little more pleasant, and it's true that for a moment anger flared across all our faces. But Kyōichi wasn't content to let the matter drop so easily. With no warning whatsoever he reached down and took off one of the heavy wooden sandals he was wearing and whammed it down on the back of the first guy's head, so forcefully that I actually heard a crack.

I was aghast.

The guy bellowed out a curse, clutched his head, and glared back at Kyōichi. Then his eyes widened in surprise, and a moment later he had scampered off into the darkness. His partners followed, pushing people aside as they dashed headlong out the main entrance and down the narrow stairway.

Everything had gone silent as goggling eyes took stock of the scene, but the silence only lasted until the young men fled, a matter of a few seconds. Soon everyone turned toward the front of the line again, and the hubbub returned.

Only the three of us remained as we were, stuck in our shock.

Finally Tsugumi broke the silence.

"Now kid, I realize that little turd was trying to push us apart, but still . . . Seriously, even I wouldn't go that far!"

Yōko and I burst out laughing.

"You don't understand," said Kyōichi. The light shining over his profile revealed a very dark expression, but his voice was more serious than anything. Still, he cheered up pretty quickly. "Actually, those assholes are responsible for this," he said, pointing to the bruise under his eye. "It all happened in the dark, and it was so sudden that I could hardly tell who had hit me, but I'm sure it was him. Serves him right."

"But what made them come after you?" I asked.

"My dad's not very popular around here. He forced folks to sell their land so that he would have a plot large enough for the hotel and stuff, you know? I mean, think about it. Some outsider comes and builds this giant hotel and sucks away all your customers . . . no one's gonna like that. My guess is that things will be pretty rough for a while. My parents and I understand that, and we're prepared for it. But I figure that after we've been here for a while, like maybe ten years or so, people will grow used to having us around."

"But none of that has anything to do with you, right?" I asked.

But even as I spoke, I found myself thinking that maybe there was something about Kyōichi that really stirred people's jealousy. He'd showed up in town with his dog, he'd been spending all this time living in an inn, all on his own, and all he did all day was go around observing the town, this town that would be his home from now on, and it had taken hardly any time at all for him to enchant the number one beauty in town—or, at any rate, the young woman who had that reputation. Eventually, that giant hotel that was being built would belong to him. There's a certain type of person in this world that just despises guys like Kyōichi. I figured that must be the problem.

"Well, I don't think there's any need to worry," said Yōko. "And I'm not just saying that because we're all going to be leaving here before long anyway, except for you—that's not what I mean. After all, our mother has really grown to like you a lot, Kyōichi. And then a couple days ago I overheard her talking with our father, and she was saying that if someone like you would be willing to stick it out here then the whole region was sure to keep getting nicer. And everyone where you're staying, over at the Nakahama Inn—I'm sure that by now they must have gotten wind of who you are. But they still make a big fuss over you, right? And they're just crazy about Gongorō! And of course you're always helping out around the inn, right? If you've managed to make this many friends in a single summer, I feel sure you'll be just fine. Once you actually start living here you'll be a local in no time."

Yōko always took so long to get to the point when she tried to explain stuff like this, and she was so utterly, almost dreadfully earnest that somehow she ended up making you want to break down crying. Kyōichi simply replied that she was probably right, and I nodded without saying anything. Tsugumi had stood facing the front of the line the entire time Yōko spoke, and she hadn't said a word, but something in her little back and in the red obi fastened around her waist told me that she was listening.

Finally our turn came. We each shook the rattle and prayed.

Tsugumi announced that since there was still time before the fireworks she wanted to go play with Gongorō, and the four of us headed down to the where Kyōichi was staying. The inn was close to the beach, so we'd be able to dash over as soon as the show started.

Gongorō was chained up in the garden. The moment he spotted Kyōichi he sprang up and started bouncing around, overjoyed. Tsugumi ran right over and started rollicking with him, not at all concerned that the bottom of her kimono was dragging all over the ground.

"Hey there!" Tsugumi cried. "Hey Gongorō!"

Yōko watched her. "So Tsugumi likes dogs after all," she sighed.

"Yeah, who would have known!" I said with a laugh.

Tsugumi turned around, looking a little annoyed.

"Sure," she snapped. "After all, a dog doesn't betray you."

"Yeah . . . I can sympathize with that," said Kyōichi. "Every so often when I'm sitting here scratching Gongorō's stomach and stuff I start thinking about that kind of thing. He's still a puppy, right, which means that he'll probably keep on eating food set out by these hands of mine until he dies—he'll probably be with me that whole time. Actually I think that's pretty amazing. He's totally there, you know, nothing can be taken away—maybe I could put it that way. You certainly can't have that with people."

"You're talking about not being betrayed?" I asked.

"I don't know . . . it's more that people can't help coming into contact with new things all the time, one thing after the next, and so bit by bit they just keep changing on you, you know? They forget all kinds of stuff, whittle stuff away, and there's nothing you can do about that—they're bound to do it. I guess it's because there are so many things for us to do, but still . . ."

"I think I see what you mean," I said.

"Yep, that's just what I meant," said Tsugumi as she continued to frolic with Gongorō. The garden of this inn had a line of flowerpots around it, lots and lots of them, and the plants in them all appeared to be extremely well cared for. There were a number of lights on in the windows, and over by the entrance we could hear the voices of people heading out to the festival or coming back, and the clip-clopping of wooden sandals on the pavement.

"The stars are pretty tonight, aren't they?"

Yōko was gazing up at the sky. With the soft glow of the Milky Way at its center, the whole wide expanse of night sky was flecked with fragments of starlight that seemed to bleed outward until they were all stuck together.

"Kyōichi, is that you out in the garden?"

I turned to look at the window from which the voice had come. It was the kitchen. A lady, evidently a member of the inn's staff, was standing there with her head outside.

"Yup, it's me!" Kyōichi replied, sounding just like a little boy.

"You have friends with you, right? I heard voices," said the lady.

"Yes, three of my friends are here."

"Well then, why don't you all snack on this." As she spoke, the lady held out a large glass plate covered with thin slices of watermelon.

"Hey, thanks a lot. I appreciate it." Kyōichi took the plate.

"It's so dark out there, why don't you all go eat in the dining room?"

"Oh no, we're fine out here. But thanks anyway." Kyōichi smiled.

We all called out our thanks and bowed lightly in the lady's direction.

She smiled back at us. "No need to thank me, just eat. Kyōichi is always helping us with all kinds of chores at the inn, after all. Can't hold it against him even if he does come from the hotel! He's a popular guy around here, you know. Hey Kyōichi, when that hotel of yours goes up you'd better be sure to send plenty of customers our way, you hear? Turn down one out of every three reservations and tell the folks that although, unfortunately, the hotel has no vacancies right now, you enthusiastically recommend the Nakahama Inn. Is that clear? You got that, Kyōichi?" said the lady.

"Ab-so-lute-ly!" said Kyōichi. "Roger!"

The lady laughed and closed the window.

Almost immediately Tsugumi reached out and took a slice of watermelon. "Kyōichi, my little lovely," she said, "you really seem to have hit it off with the old hags. You must be one of these old-lady-killers you hear about, huh?"

"I bet you could find a more pleasant way to say that if you tried," said Yōko. But Tsugumi's expression remained utterly unconcerned, and she kept eating her watermelon. Beads of sweat were trickling down her face.

"Do you really help them that much?" I asked. I'd never heard of a guest helping out with the work at an inn.

"Yeah, I don't really have much else to do with my time, so somehow I just end up working. They seem to be understaffed, and it gets incredibly busy every morning, and then again at night. Of course in return for my labor they're letting me keep Gongorō with me, and they give me food." Kyōichi grinned.

I got the feeling that Aunt Masako was right. Things would be fine as long as Kyōichi was here, even after the rest of us had gone.

The watermelon was a little watery, but it was sweet and not overly strong. We gobbled down slice after slice, squatting there in the dark. The water from the hose we used to wash our hands was very cold—it formed a tiny river on the dark soil and trickled away. At first Gongorō had been watching us eat, an envious expression on his face, but after a while he rolled his small body over in a patch of grass and lay there. He shut his eyes.

We see all kinds of different things as we grow up. And with each instant that passes we change into something new. We keep moving forward, and as we move we keep being confronted by this fact, over and over again, in many different ways. But if there were one thing that I wanted to hold on to even with this knowledge, to retain just as it was, it would be this evening. I didn't need anything else, I didn't need anything more—that's how happy we were then, how full the air surrounding us was with a small and quiet joy.

* * *

"This summer is the best ever!" said Kyōichi.

"Watermelon is the most delicious thing in the world!" said Tsugumi.

I suppose she meant this as an answer to Kyōichi's comment.

Soon a sudden boom rippled through the sky. We heard cheers.

"The fireworks have started!" Tsugumi leapt up, her eyes shining.

Looking up, we saw an enormous globe of fireworks blossom in the shadow of the inn and continue to expand, growing wider and wider. We ran for the beach, chasing the booms that began a moment later.

The sky over the ocean was wide open, with nothing to obstruct our view, and it was strange to see the fireworks unfurling way up there, like lights from outer space. The four of us sat in a line on the beach, hardly speaking at all, gazing up at the unfolding sequence of fireworks, enchanted.

Rage

When Tsugumi really gets furious it's like she turns to ice.

Of course this only happens when she gets really, really mad. Tsugumi is constantly losing her temper over one thing or another, turning bright red and running around yelling her lungs out at everyone within range, but that's not the kind of anger I mean. It's when she fixes someone with a look of absolute hatred, like she despises the person from the very bottom of her soul—at times like that she turns into a completely different person. Everything but her hatred fades from her mind, and her whole body takes on the blue-white tint of rage. Whenever I see her like that, I find myself thinking about stars. I remember hearing that, as they grow hotter and hotter, the light they emit shifts from a reddish hue to an increasingly clear blue-white. In all the years I've been around Tsugumi, I've hardly ever seen her that mad.

I think this must have been just after Tsugumi moved up into junior high. Yōko and Tsugumi and I were all in the same school, each in a different grade. Yōko was in ninth, I was in eighth, and Tsugumi was in seventh.

It was during lunch. Rain was pouring down outside, making everything seem drab and gloomy. We couldn't go outside, so all the students were fooling around in the classrooms. Sudden outbursts of laughter, the noises of people dashing through the halls, a shrill scream . . . rainwater streaming violently down all the classroom windows, almost like a waterfall . . . The riotous commotion of noise resounded through the claustrophobic darkness, near and distant, like the sound of the ocean.

All of a sudden the sharp whack of shattering glass—

Cra-a-ck-k-crash!

slammed through the uproar. The noises in the room all snapped into silence for a second, but then an even greater commotion broke out. Someone went out into the hall to see what was going on, and shouted in that whatever was happening was out on the terrace. We had all been bored out of our minds, and we were so quick to herd ourselves out of the room that it could have been a race. The terrace was at the end of the hall on the second floor: there was this glass door that led out and then a bunch of little pots for growing plants in science class, a rabbit hutch, a stack of extra chairs, that kind of thing. As I trailed along casually at the rear of the crowd it occurred to me that maybe the crash we'd heard had been the sound of that glass door breaking.

I peered up ahead through the boisterous crowd—and boy did I get a shock! Standing by herself in the middle of a field of broken glass, looking as if she would never budge an inch, was Tsugumi.

Suddenly she spoke. "Did that prove how strong I am, huh?

Or do you want me to do some more?" Her tone was almost entirely flat, but you could sense how much strength she was putting into her words. I followed her gaze to a girl standing nearby, her face dreadfully pale. They were in the same class. She was Tsugumi's worst enemy.

Turning to a girl who was standing nearby, I hurriedly questioned her about what had happened. She said she wasn't quite sure but that Tsugumi had been chosen to represent the class in some marathon, and when she said she couldn't run, this other girl had been selected to run in her place. The other girl was really annoyed about being chosen after Tsugumi, and the rumor was that she'd asked Tsugumi to step out into the hall during recess and then made some sort of sarcastic comment. At which point, without saying a word, Tsugumi had picked up a nearby chair and hurled it into the glass. That was the story.

"Try repeating what you said earlier!" said Tsugumi.

The girl couldn't reply. All around me people were holding their breath, gulping nervously. No one even went to get a teacher. Tsugumi seemed to have cut herself slightly when she broke the glass—there was a little blood on her ankle—but she didn't seem to care. She kept gazing straight at the girl. And then I noticed how terrifying the look in her eyes was. The fear you felt looking into them wasn't like the feeling that came over us when we saw the tough guys at school, it was like she was insane. Her eyes glittered quietly as if she were staring off into some space that had no limits, that went on forever.

Thinking back on that incident now, I kind of get the feeling that Tsugumi changed after that day—maybe this was when she started keeping her true self hidden at school. This was to be the last time Tsugumi ever made a scene in public. But I bet that for the rest of their lives, none of the people present will ever forget the way she was then. The intense light that radiated from her body, an energy in her eyes that rose from a hatred so deep you felt sure it would drive her to kill the girl, or herself.

I shoved my way through the ring of people and stepped into the clearing. Tsugumi's gaze shot briefly in my direction—the look in her eyes made it clear she saw me as nothing but an interference. For a moment I felt something within me hesitate, yearning to retreat.

"Tsugumi, that's enough. Let it go," I said. I figured she probably wanted someone to make her back away—even she had no idea what to do next. The spectators got even tenser when I appeared, making me feel like a matador dancing out in front of a bull. "Come on, Tsugumi. Let's go home."

I reached out and took Tsugumi's arm in my hand, and felt a wave of shock shudder through me. Her eyes stared back into mine very coolly, but her skin was burning up. She was so enraged that she had actually started running a fever. The shock made me fall silent. Suddenly, with a quick, harsh movement, Tsugumi shook off my hand. A burst of anger shot up inside me and I made an effort to grab hold of her arm again, but just then the girl she was fighting with whirled around on her heel and fled.

"Damn you, wait!" cried Tsugumi.

I fought to hold Tsugumi back and she struggled to get away, and it began to seem as if a new fight was about to break out, this time between the two of us. But just then Yōko made her entrance at the top of the stairs, walking slowly toward us. "Tsugumi, what on earth are you doing?" she asked.

Tsugumi must have decided that there was nothing she could do anymore, because all of a sudden she stopped thrashing. She used one of her hands to push me slowly back. Yōko glanced around at the shards of glass and the circle of people, and then let her eyes play over my face.

"What's been happening here, Maria?" she asked, her face registering a complex mixture of embarrassment, confusion, and annoyance.

But I couldn't answer. It seemed like no matter what I said, I would end up wounding Tsugumi. The fight had started as a result of some comment the other girl had made about her body, and I could understand how desperately, humiliatingly angry that must have made her.

"Well, you see . . ." I mumbled. But Tsugumi cut me off.

"Shut up," she said quietly. "It's none of your business!" Her voice was terribly barren. She seemed as if she no longer held even a fragment of hope. She quietly kicked at a few pieces of glass, sending them scattering. The dull tinkle echoed down the hall.

"Tsugumi—" began Yōko, but Tsugumi clutched at her head and shook it back and forth as if to say, *Would you shut up already!* and she kept doing this with such ferocity that it almost seemed as if blood would start streaming from her skin, so Yōko and I made her stop. Tsugumi abandoned her struggle and went into her classroom, and then emerged again, carrying her backpack. She walked right down the stairs and went home.

The students who had been watching dispersed, the glass was cleared away, and Yōko went to apologize to Tsugumi's teacher. I headed back to my own classroom, the bell rang, and class started just as if nothing had happened. Only my hand still felt hot, burning with a steady pain as if it had fallen asleep. It was Tsugumi's fever, still burning in my hand. It was a strange sensation. The heat didn't seem at all inclined to leave, but kept burning on and on like some afterimage, an echo, oddly bright. I sat very still, gazing at my prickling palm, and thought for ages and ages about how Tsugumi's anger had a life of its own, how anger streamed through her body like blood.

"Gongoro's gone. I think someone's taken him."

Kyōichi had only asked if Tsugumi was home, but the voice that came over the phone was so urgent and grim that I had asked him if anything was wrong. An image of the guys we'd run into at the shrine—the ones who hated Kyōichi so much—slid briefly, nastily through my mind.

"What makes you think that?" I asked.

I felt a sense of panic welling up through my chest.

"His leash was cut," Kyōichi said, trying to sound calm.

"Oh no!" I cried. "Listen, I'm going to come right over, okay? Tsugumi's not home right now, she's at the hospital for a checkup, but I'll leave a message with someone here before I go. Where are you now?"

"The pay phone at the entrance to the beach."

"Okay, just stay put! I'll be right there!" I said, and hung up.

I asked Aunt Masako to tell Tsugumi what had happened, then went up to Yōko's room and dragged her out of her futon, where she'd been sound asleep. I explained the situation as the two of us ran out the door. Kyōichi was standing by the phone. His expression softened just a little when he saw us, but his eyes remained hard.

"Okay, let's split up and search different areas," said Yōko.

The sight of Kyōichi must have made her realize how serious this was.

"All right then, I'll head into town, so why don't the two of you go around the beach," said Kyōichi. "If you should run into any of the assholes who took Gongorō, just come right back here without saying a word to them, you got that? Man, he was barking like crazy, you know, and I thought it was kinda strange, but by the time I got outside, he was gone. It's pretty fucking annoying, let me tell you."

Kyōichi ran off down the narrow road that leads to town.

Yōko and I split up and hurried off to the right and the left, using the long concrete dike that stretches out into the ocean midway down the beach as our marker. Already night was closing in. A few stars had started twinkling in the sky, and with each passing moment another layer of blue cloth joined the pile that tinted the air. My sense of panic grew stronger, and I started shouting Gongorō's name. I ran and ran, calling him again and again, from the top of the bridge at the end of the river, from inside the little thicket of pine trees, but no barking ever answered my shouts. I wanted to cry. Every time I stopped and stood struggling to catch my breath, the world around me would darken, and I'd see the enormous ocean stretching hazily away into the distance. *Even if Gongorō were out there drowning, I'd never know it in this dark,* I thought, getting even more desperate than before.

By the time we returned to the dike at the middle of the beach, Yōko and I were both completely exhausted, dripping with sweat. We agreed to split up and search once more, but before going we went and stood at the tip of the dike and yelled out Gongorō's name in unison. Both the ocean and the shore were dark now; they had been reborn as a single space of darkness, and it felt as if this vast dark had enveloped our tiny arms and legs in its enormous folds, swallowed them down in a single gulp. The beam of the lighthouse swept around in our direction at even intervals, then swung back out over the ocean.

"I guess we'd better have another look," I sighed. But then, glancing over in the direction of the shore, I caught sight of a single dot of light, so strong it seemed almost like a searchlight, pressing through the dark haze of the evening, heading our way over the bridge. Slowly, surefootedly, it cut across the beach. "You know, I have a feeling that's Tsugumi," I murmured. But my voice was lost amidst the sound of the waves.

"What?"

Yōko's hair tangled in the wind, glinting in the dark, as she turned.

"See that light over there, coming this way? I think it's Tsugumi."

"Where?" Yōko squinted. She focused on the spot of light on the beach. "I can't tell if it's her or not. It's too far away."

"I bet it's Tsugumi." I really did have that feeling. After all, the light was headed straight for us—what else was there to think? With no sense of doubt at all in my mind, I shouted her name.

"Tsugumi!"

I waved vigorously in the dark.

And off in the distance the flashlight traced two circles. Just as I'd thought, it was Tsugumi! Soon the beam turned slowly out onto the dike. When she made it to the bend, we finally succeeded in making out her small form.

Tsugumi remained silent as she approached. She marched powerfully on in our direction, so alive with energy that she almost seemed to slash through the darkness. The flashlight's beam glimmered vaguely across her pale face. She was biting her lips. Then I saw her eyes, and realized how angry she was. Her left hand held the inn's largest flashlight. I saw Gongorō squirming about under her right arm. He was drenched, and looked a size smaller than usual.

"You found him!" I darted over, so thrilled that I almost started jumping. A wide smile spread across Yōko's face as well.

"Yeah, over on the far side of the bridge," grunted Tsugumi. She handed me the flashlight, then used her skinny arms to scoot Gongorō around into a better position. "He was in the river, paddling like mad."

"I'll get Kyōichi!" cried Yōko, and ran off toward the beach.

"You, Maria, collect some wood," Tsugumi ordered, still hugging Gongorō. "We're gonna make a fire and dry this guy."

"We can't make a bonfire, Tsugumi, we'll get in trouble. Let's just go back to the inn and have someone get out one of the kerosene heaters," I said.

"Listen, kid, with this much water around I think we'll be all right. And if you used your head at all you'd realize that if we went back like this the old hag would bawl me out so bad I wouldn't know what hit me," said Tsugumi. "Try swinging that light in my direction, darling."

I obeyed, aiming the beam of the flashlight over her way just as she'd said, and got a very major shock. She was totally drenched from the waist down. Drops of water were raining down onto the concrete.

"Oh great," I moaned. "What part of the river was he in?"

"A part of the river deep enough that you should be able to tell just from looking at me, you ass," Tsugumi snapped.

"All right, all right. I'll go get some wood!" I said.

And I ran off toward the beach.

At first Gongorō was scared out of his wits, and for a long time he just sat there shivering, his whole body stiff, but eventually he calmed down a bit and started padding around the edge of the fire.

"This guy here has no problem with fire. We always take him along with us when my family goes camping and stuff, you know, so he's gotten used to campfires like this." There was a tender gleam in Kyōichi's eyes as he said this. His face was bathed in light from the fire.

Yōko and I nodded. We were crouched down beside each other. The fire was small, but the warmth it gave was just right for a slightly chilly night like this, a night when the wind was strong. Firelight flickered out across the dark troughs of water that hung between the waves.

Tsugumi remained standing, saying nothing. Her skirt had finally started to dry out a little, but even so it was tinted dark and clung to her legs. And yet she didn't seem particularly aware of this—she just went on staring into the flames, reaching down again and again to toss the broken boards and pieces of driftwood I had collected onto the fire. She has such huge eyes and her skin glimmered so whitely that it was frightening, and I couldn't bring myself to speak to her.

"He's gotten pretty dry, hasn't he?" said Yōko, stroking Gongorō.

"I'll take him back home the day after tomorrow," said Kyōichi.

"What? You're going home?" I asked.

Tsugumi gave a start, and looked up.

"Nah, I'm just gonna go leave the dog," said Kyōichi. "With stuff like this happening it worries me to leave him at the inn. So I won't."

"Why the day after tomorrow?" asked Yōko.

"My parents are away on a trip right now. There won't be anyone at home until then," said Kyōichi.

"Well then, I've got an idea!" said Yōko. "Why don't we put Gongorō in Pooch's doghouse at the house behind the inn? That way we know he'll be safe until you take him back!"

"Right, I like that idea!" I said.

"It would be a big help if you could do that," said Kyōichi.

Suddenly all of us around the fire felt better, friendlier, warmer.

Kyōichi glanced up at Tsugumi, who was still standing. "Hey Tsugumi," he said, "I'll come get you in the morning, and we'll go for a walk, okay? It'll be easier having both dogs in the same place, anyway."

"Yeah," Tsugumi replied, and gave a faint smile. We got a tiny glimpse of her white teeth, illuminated by the flickering of the fire. She stood there in the dark with her small childlike hands stretched out over the flames, her long eyelashes casting shadows on her cheeks. And yet even so I had the feeling that she was angry. It was the first time in her life that Tsugumi had gotten angry on someone else's behalf. Something about her felt sacred to me then. "You know, if this kind of thing ever happens again," she muttered, "even if it's after we've moved, I'll come back here and I'll kill them."

As violent as her words were, her eyes were still just as lucid as they had been, and her expression remained very mild. Her tone had been so entirely ordinary that for a while none of us was able to speak.

Finally Kyōichi said, "That's an idea, Tsugumi."

I listened to the echo of that final word, *Tsugumi,* as it vanished delicately into the waves. The night had deepened, and there were tons of stars out. We hadn't told anyone at home where we were, and we wouldn't—we stayed there at the tip of the dike, caught up in a mood that wouldn't let us leave. Each one of us was equally fond of Gongorō, each one of us thought of him as irreplaceable. And maybe Gongorō had sensed that? Because he kept trotting from one of us to the next, from one to the next, sniffing at things and putting his paws up on our knees, licking our faces. Little by little he seemed to be forgetting the terrible thing that had happened to him. A strong wind was blowing, and every so often the flames of the fire began whipping wildly back and forth, seeming almost on the verge of expiring, but each time Tsugumi would toss on another piece of wood, just as casually as if she were throwing away a scrap of trash, and the fire would grow. The crackling of the burning wood mingled with the sounds of the waves and the wind, and it was as if the sound were being blown away into the darkness at our backs. And the ocean continued to roll its black, sleek surface onward toward the shore.

"I'm glad you're okay, buddy," said Yōko, putting an arm around Gongorō's as he eagerly fidgeted, and scooping him up from her lap, where he had climbed yet again. She rose to her feet and stood staring out across the distant waves, her long hair swishing back and forth across her back. "Boy, this wind sure is strong, isn't it!" she said. "It won't be long until autumn now."

Summer is almost over.

This knowledge left us a little quieter than before. For a moment I found myself wishing, really wishing that Tsugumi's clothes would never ever dry, that our fire would never die.

The next day Kyōichi came to tell us that he'd found one of the guys who made off with Gongorō in town, and dragged him up to the shrine and given him one hell of a thrashing. He was pretty banged up himself, but Tsugumi was thrilled to hear the news. Yōko and I helped Kyōichi fix up his wounds. Gongorō was sleeping with Pooch out in the garden, the two of them now just as chummy as could be.

One more day and Gongorō could have returned home. Just a single day more would have been enough.

But that night someone made off with him again. It happened while the four of us were out. Aunt Masako said she heard him barking and ran outside, only to find the gate open and Gongorō gone. Left on his own, Pooch went on jangling his chain and jumping around in a panic.

We sprinted to the shore, feeling this time like we really were going to burst crying. The four of us walked up and down the beach until late that night, covering every square foot, and went out in a boat and shone lights into the water, and asked friends to search the river and hunt through town.

But luck wasn't with us this time. Gongorō never came back.

The Hole

"You'll come back here before I leave, won't you?" said Tsugumi, staring at Kyōichi with paralyzed eyes. Her face had that look on it that people get when they're struggling to hold back tears—the saddest expression in the world.

"Of course. I'll only be gone two or three days." Kyōichi laughed.

Seeing him on the beach now without Gongorō to complete the pair, you had the impression that his body was lopsided, off-balance, like a person missing a limb. And in a way it was true—here in this still-unfamiliar town, Kyōichi really had lost a part of himself.

"Yeah, I see your point. I mean, you're not a kid anymore, huh? It's not like you won't be able to leave your parents," said Tsugumi.

Evening was drawing closer, and rays of sun played across the surface of the ocean, flooding it with gold. Tsugumi and Kyōichi walked side by side, making their way along the dike that traced the shore, heading for the harbor. They talked as they walked, and Yōko and I followed behind, watching them. We were on our way to see Kyōichi off. Yōko was already getting ready to cry, and I felt strangely absent. Autumn wind blew quietly over my cheeks.

Next week I'll be heading back to Tokyo.

How many times this summer have I looked out over an ocean like this? Just like always. Flooded with so much light, a final breath of sunshine flaring up over the western horizon, disappearing little by little, never glancing back, into the haze of darkness—this ocean.

The harbor was bustling, echoing with the noise of people waiting for the last ferry of the day, which was scheduled to arrive in a few minutes. Kyōichi dropped his bag with a *whump* and sat down on top of it, then called Tsugumi over and had her sit down next to him. I felt a hint of loneliness in the shape of their backs as they sat together looking out over the distant ocean, and yet somehow that shape also seemed imbued with an unyielding strength. The combination reminded me of a dog waiting for its master.

The sharp waves that announce the coming of autumn were still shining out there in all their overlapping brilliance. In this season each tiny glimpse I get of the ocean calls up an ache so tender it's like having ropes bound around my heart, cutting into the flesh. But this year the pain stabbed at me more ferociously than I would ever have expected. Without even realizing it was happening, this farewell of theirs had me pressing my fingers to my temples, kicking scraps of bait that lay scattered on the pavement at my feet down into the water, fighting to hold back tears.

Because even though Tsugumi just kept saying the same things and asking the same questions, repeating herself so often that it got a bit cloying—*When will you be back?* she'd say, and, *If you've got time to sit around talking on the phone, you might as well just get on the train and come yourself, you know? Even if it's just a day ear-lier*—her tone was still deeply touching. Tsugumi's translucent voice seemed to mingle with the crashing of the waves to create a music that was strangely beautiful.

"We may not be together, but don't forget me," Tsugumi muttered, almost as if she were speaking to herself. "Don't ever forget me."

The ferry arrived exactly as it always does—beelining in from the horizon, pushing up waves. Tsugumi rose, and Kyōichi shoul-dered his bag.

"Well, see you around," he said, turning to face Yōko and me. "Come to think of it, Maria, rumor has it that you'll be heading home soon, too. We might end up just missing each other, huh? We'll be in touch, though. You gotta come stay in our hotel when it's finished."

"Sure. You'll give me a good deal, right?" I said, holding out my hand.

"Naturally," he said.

My summer pal put his warm hand around mine and shook it.

"I've got an idea, Kyōichi. Why don't you marry me, right, and then we'll fill the garden of the hotel with dogs and call it 'Dog Palace'? How's that sound to you?" asked Tsugumi ingenuously.

"Yeah . . . I'll think about it." Kyōichi smiled wryly. Next he held out his hand to Yōko, who was halfway in tears. "Thanks for everything," he said.

The boat's gangway created a bridge with the land, and people moved into line and began to stream into the boat, one after the other after the other.

Kyōichi looked at Tsugumi. "Well, see you soon."

"If you even try and shake my hand I'll break your spine!" cried Tsugumi, throwing herself around his neck.

It only lasted an instant. Without even wiping away the tears that streamed down her cheeks, Tsugumi shoved Kyōichi toward the boat. Kyōichi didn't say anything. He just gazed long and hard at Tsugumi, then ran off after the last person in line and boarded the boat.

The whistle blew and the boat started moving, heading slowly out toward the ocean and the sky, the line between which was growing ever more vague. Kyōichi stood on the deck, waving and waving his hand. Tsugumi crouched down and watched the boat slide away without even returning his wave.

The boat passed completely out of sight.

"Tsugumi," said Yōko.

"Ladies and gentlemen, this concludes the ceremony!" cried Tsugumi, and stood up. The expression on her face was so nonchalant it was as if nothing had happened. "I mean what the hell, the big booby goes running home just 'cause his dog died. You can say we're grown up and whatever else you like, but we're all still nineteen or thereabouts, huh? We might as well be a bunch of little brats on summer vacation."

She'd said this in a murmur, not aiming it at anyone in particular, but her words caught the vague idea that had been circling through my head.

"You said it," I agreed.

For a while after that the three of us stood in silence at the very edge of the harbor, as if we were in the closing scene of some movie, staring out over the farther reaches of the ocean and at the coloring of the sky as it reflected the sun, which had now sunk utterly from view.

Five days passed, and still Kyōichi hadn't come back. Apparently Tsugumi was so mad that every time he called she'd just hang up on him.

I was in my room working on an essay that I had to turn in after classes started again when there was a knock at my door, and Yōko came in.

"What's up?" I asked.

"Listen, Maria, do you have any idea where Tsugumi's been going these last few nights, after it gets late?" Yōko asked. "She's gone now, too."

"You don't think she's just gone on a walk?" I asked. Tsugumi had been very irritable since Kyōichi left, and recently her mood had turned so ugly that you could hardly believe it. Every time I started feeling sorry for her and tried to be nice she'd turn around and take it all out on me, so I'd been keeping my distance, letting her do as she pleased.

"Pooch is still in his doghouse," Yōko said, looking worried.

"Oh, is he?" I cocked my head slightly. Usually I could never make any sense at all of Tsugumi's actions, but this time I had something of a hunch. "Well, I'll ask her if I have a chance."

Yōko nodded and left the room as soon as I'd said this.

Why do all these people fail to understand Tsugumi—why do they misread her character like this? Kyōichi and Yōko were both completely convinced by Tsugumi's pantomimed dejection. True, she had acted the part extremely well, making it seem as if the sadness in her really had beaten out the hatred. But Tsugumi isn't the kind of person who just sits around twiddling her thumbs when a dog she's fond of is murdered. It was revenge. That was the only possible explanation for these excursions of hers. *She's such an idiot, she really is! Her body is too delicate for her to be getting involved in stuff like this,* I thought, and for an instant I was seriously annoyed. But still I couldn't tell Yōko.

Apparently Tsugumi was back now, because I heard noises in the next room. Then, mixed in with the other sounds, came the yipping of a dog.

"Tsugumi? What are you doing?" I said, walking over to the door of her bedroom and sliding it open. "Are you bringing Pooch inside? You know that when Aunt Masako finds out she'll whack you so hard you—"

Having said this much, I fell silent. I was stunned. Of course it couldn't be Gongorō—he was dead, after all—but it was precisely the same breed of dog, and it looked so similar to Gongorō that for a moment I was dreadfully shaken. "Wh-what's going on here?" I stammered.

"I borrowed him. Gotta give him back soon, but hey." Tsugumi grinned. "I just felt so lonely without a dog around, you know?"

"You're such a liar," was all I said. I went and sat down next to Tsugumi and started thinking furiously, even as I petted the dog in front of me. It had been a while since I'd last relished the taste of a struggle like this. When things started progressing in this direction you either had to figure out what Tsugumi was planning, or she'd shut her mouth and refuse to say another word.

"For starters, you're planning on parading this dog in front of the guys who killed Gongorō, right?" I asked.

"Wow, babe, nice work! You really are pretty clever, huh?" said Tsugumi, flashing me a little grin. "Without you around, it's just all these bozos who can never understand what I'm thinking. It really wears me out."

"Tsugumi," I said, laughing, "no one understands what you're thinking."

"Wanna hear about tonight?" Tsugumi said, picking up the dog.

"I'd love to." I was leaning toward her now. It doesn't matter how many years pass, at times like this we both turn into children again, sharing a secret. Suddenly the night seems to grow more dense, and we feel giddy.

"I've spent these last few days investigating the weedy little assholes, pint-sized punks that they are, trying to find out what kind of group they belong to. You noticed I haven't been around at night?"

"I'd noticed."

"Well, turns out they're nothing much. They look old, but they're all just high school kids. Local losers, in other words. They hang out at this snack bar in the next town over."

"And you went there, Tsugumi?"

"Yup, that's where I was tonight. And man was I scared. My hands were trembling." Tsugumi showed me her palms. Her hands weren't trembling, they were just extremely small and white. I stared at her palms, feeling a quiet stirring of emotion, and listened as she continued to talk.

"So I climb up the stairs to the snack bar, right, holding this little guy in my arms. The place is on the second floor. Now, the assholes in question are low-down little pieces of crap, I'll give them that much, but there's no way any of them would have the courage to go out and dirty his own hands, actually kill a dog. I'm guessing they just dropped Gongorō into the ocean, you know, maybe tied some sort of weight or something to him first, but that's the farthest they'd go. So I don't think they saw him die. I'm pretty sure of that."

My eyes still went dark when I thought of what had been done to Gongorō. Even before the anger came, everything turned black.

"It was enough just to give them a glimpse of this dog. Of course it would be pretty damn bad if there were a whole lot of them, and if they actually came after me . . . well, that'd be the end of the story, huh? As tough as I am, I gotta tell you, Maria—I was really scared shitless when I opened that door. But I did it anyway. Luckily there was only one of them sitting at the counter, and he was a guy I'd definitely seen before. The bozo glanced back and forth from me to the dog with this sort of startled, frightened look in his eyes, and I gave him this really nasty look, and then very quickly I turned my back on him and slammed the door behind me as hard as I could and dashed down the stairs. I figured that if I had to try to run from him he was bound to catch me, so I got down behind the stairs to hide. Fortunately the idiot just opened the door and then closed it again, that was it. But man, during the time he was standing up there my legs were shaking like you wouldn't believe."

"Sounds pretty wild."

"It was. I'm running a fever." Tsugumi smiled as if this were something to be proud of. "It's funny, I have the idea that when I was kid I put myself in this much danger every day. Guess I've gone soft, huh?"

"I don't care if you're going soft or whatever, your body isn't strong enough for you to go around doing things like this," I said. "You can't put something like this on the same level as the stupid stuff kids do to show how tough they are."

Still, I did feel a bit relieved now that she'd told me the story.

"Okay, I'm going to sleep now," said Tsugumi, climbing halfway down into her futon. "Would you mind tying this little guy up outside for me? The jerks might come take him if you put him with Pooch, so you better leave him under the veranda or something."

Tsugumi really looked exhausted, so I nodded and scooped up the dog, and then stood up. I buried my face in the hair of his small head, and then, almost before I realized what I was saying, I blurted out, "He even smells like Gongorō!"

Tsugumi said quietly that I was right, he did.

My room was pitch dark, and I was fast asleep.

In my dream I had a faint sense of some noise, off in the distance. I rolled over in my futon with a groan, turning to face the door, and suddenly realized what the sounds were. It was someone sobbing, and mingled with these sobs the heavy *clump clump clump* of feet ascending the stairs.

The awful sense of unreality that hit me, the fear I extracted from the dark, finally succeeded in waking me. With my mind clear, I became increasingly conscious of the fact that the noises were headed in my direction, and for one nightmarish instant I found myself unable to figure out where this place was, where I had woken up, and when. Then my eyes adjusted to the darkness, and I saw my feet and hands and the white of my blanket resting dimly in the black.

Then the sound of a door sliding open.

The realization that whatever was happening was happening in Tsugumi's room threw me into a state of confusion. This time I really was completely awake, so I got out of my futon and stood up. Then I heard a voice.

"Tsugumi!"

It was Yōko. I stepped out into the dark hall and stood there peering into Tsugumi's room. The door was open, and Yōko was standing inside.

Tsugumi's room gets quite a lot of moonlight. Tsugumi was sitting up on her futon, and I could see her wide-open eyes shining whitely in the darkness. Following her gaze, I saw Yōko—her entire body was plastered in mud. She was trembling, staring fixedly at Tsugumi, sobbing wildly, gulping down her breath. These hiccuplike gasps truly seemed to have frightened Tsugumi—that was how she looked—and she sat there completely frozen.

"Yōko, what . . . ?" I said. I had the horrifying idea that maybe she had been attacked by those guys. But she spoke quietly.

"Tsugumi, you know what I've just been doing, don't you?"

Slowly, without saying a word, Tsugumi nodded.

"You just can't do stuff like that!" Yōko cried, wiping her face with one of her filthy hands. Then, pouring all the energy she had into her words, which were interrupted even so by her continuing hiccup-sobs, she said, "You simply won't be able to get along in life if you're going to do stuff like that!"

I hadn't the foggiest idea what she was talking about. I went on standing there, looking at the two sisters as they faced off in the dark, not even thinking to switch on the lights. Suddenly Tsugumi lowered her eyes, then reached down and violently snatched up the towel that lay under her pillow—had she gotten this idea from Kyōichi's story?—and thrust it out toward Yōko.

". . . I'm sorry."

It must be something pretty bad if Tsugumi's apologizing! I thought, catching my breath. Yōko nodded very slightly and accepted the towel. She wiped away her tears as she left the room. I watched Tsugumi dive under the cover of her futon, and then, since there wasn't really much else I could do, hurried after Yōko, who was heading down the stairs.

"What happened?" I cried. My voice echoed so loudly in the dark hall that I was taken aback. "Are you okay?" I asked, lowering my voice.

"Yes, I'm fine," replied Yōko, and gave me a smile . . . or, rather, since it was too dark for me to be able to tell whether or not she'd actually smiled, a half-perceptible hint that she had reached me through the dark. "Tell me, what do you think Tsugumi used that dog for?"

"What? But I tied it up under the veranda earlier!"

"You were tricked, Maria." At this point, Yōko couldn't suppress a chuckle. "Now I know what Tsugumi has been doing all these nights."

"But wasn't she trying to track down those guys?" I asked. Then suddenly something occurred to me. Surely Tsugumi could have checked up on that snack bar in the next town by telephone.

"She was digging a hole," said Yōko.

"Huh?" I cried, raising my voice again.

Yōko motioned for me to follow her into her room.

Now that we were finally in a room with lights, all the things that had just taken place in the dark seemed to spiral away dizzily into the world of dreams. Yōko was totally plastered with mud, but when I suggested that she'd better run and take a bath first she just shook her head and told me to listen. "I've had a genuine adventure," she said. And then she told me the story of the hole.

"It was an amazing hole. Really deep.

"I simply can't imagine how she managed to dig a hole like that, and what she did with all the dirt. I suppose she must have worked on it every night after we were all asleep, that must be it, and then when morning came she'd place a board over the top and cover it with dirt . . .

"So anyway, I was fast asleep, you know? And then all of a sudden I just woke up, I'm not really sure why, and I was lying there listening in the dark. And then I kind of got this tiny little flicker of a feeling like I'd heard someone groaning. It made me really scared, and I started thinking that maybe I'd just imagined it because of it being night and all, but it was so . . . it sounded like it was coming from the garden, so I went out to see what it was. I'm sure you know the feeling, right? How the sort of thrill of doing things like that sort of lures you on. I opened the gate—it was pitch dark out, and I'd gone out without a flashlight, just groping my way around, but I had this feeling that it wasn't coming from our house. It was the house around back, where Pooch lives. I started thinking that maybe robbers had broken in and the family was in there tied up or something, except that Pooch had never started barking . . . and since I was thinking about that I decided that first of all I had better go take a look at Pooch, see how he was—that's why I was opening the gate. So I walked on through, and then the moment I got into the garden—you know how it is in the dark? How you can smell things so clearly? Well, there was this really intense odor of freshly turned soil, much stronger than usual. And so I was standing there with my head cocked slightly to one side, and then I heard the groan . . . It was coming from inside the ground. I could hardly believe that it was true, you know, so I bent down and put my ear to the ground to make sure, and kept listening to it again and again, just to make sure. Gradually my eyes got used to the dark, and so I looked more closely around where Pooch should be—and let me tell you, what I saw gave me a shock. Because Gongorō was there, too. Somehow without even noticing I had stumbled into some place that wasn't part of reality, that's really how it seemed . . . except that when I looked more carefully I realized that the color of this dog was subtly different, and for some reason both dogs had these sort of gaglike things in their mouths. I had no idea at all what to do, or what was going on, but to begin with I went and got a flashlight and shone it on the ground. And when I did, I realized that the earth right in front of the doghouse was different from all the rest, so I ran off and rustled up a shovel and dug away like crazy at the ground there. After a while this thick board appeared. I banged on the board with the handle of the shovel, and there was a groan. From then on I worked absolutely desperately. I got down and used every last drop of my strength to drag the board away and then aimed the flashlight down the hole. It was incredibly narrow and deep, and there was this guy at the bottom. Can you imagine how terrifying that was for me? The guy had duct tape over his mouth, and there was blood on his forehead, and his hands were all covered in mud and he was stetching them up toward me. Then it dawned on me that he was one of the guys in the group that had made off with Gongorō, and as soon as I'd gotten that far Tsugumi's face flew into my mind. I understood then that this was all Tsugumi's doing. I had a terrible time dragging the guy up out of the hole—I could reach him with my hands, but he kept sliding back down again. That's how deep the hole was. So as you can see I got totally plastered in mud, but somehow I did manage to get him out, and I peeled the tape away from his mouth. And now that I could really see him I realized that he was just a kid. He looked like he was probably still in high school. And he had this look on his face like he was about to start crying, and we were both so exhausted that we didn't even speak, we just collapsed onto the ground and sat there. Of course it's not as if there was anything for us to say. And then I was thinking about Tsugumi. About all the different things that have happened since she was small. And I just started feeling so sad—I stood there in the dark garden, gazing down into that deep hole that Tsugumi had dug, and my tears just wouldn't stop. And while I was like that, still in a daze, the guy wandered out through the gate, and then I started thinking, *Gosh, I have to do something about this hole.* For the time being I just put the board back and covered it with dirt . . . then I came inside."

After she finished telling her story, Yōko headed downstairs to the inn's large bath, taking a change of clothes. My head was now buzzing with all sorts of different things, and I was still in a daze when I went back to my room. I hesitated for a moment as I passed Tsugumi's door, struggling to make up my mind whether I ought to go in or not, but in the end I decided not to.

It had occurred to me that she might be feeling so miserable about all this and about everything that she was in there crying herself.

Tsugumi is never careless about anything—she's always terribly thorough. It made my head whirl just to imagine how tremendously difficult the task she had carried out those nights must have been, and how fatigued she must be.

Night after night, late enough that none of us would notice, Tsugumi had been out there digging that hole. Hauling out the dirt, constantly worrying that someone might discover her, in a garden that belonged to someone else. Digging that hole. And during the same period of time she'd been wandering around the town searching for a dog that looked like Gongorō. Maybe she'd sweet-talked the dog's owner into letting her borrow it, maybe she'd bought it. Next she told me about the adventure she'd had earlier that night, acting as if that was the whole plan— pulling the wool over my eyes had been the work of an instant, it didn't even require any planning—and had me tie the dog to the veranda so that I wouldn't start wondering. Because I'm always the most suspicious, and I tend to sense things like this even before they happen. Tsugumi went out into the garden afterward and gagged the two dogs so they wouldn't bark at the intruder when he arrived, and removed the board that she'd used both to camouflage the hole and to prevent other people from falling down inside, replacing it with a thin sheet of cardboard or something along those lines, and thus transforming it into an actual activated booby trap. The whole plan would probably have gone to pieces if they had come as a gang. Maybe she'd gone to that snack bar at a time when she knew only one member of the group would be there. And no doubt she had been out there watching, waiting for the guy, without even being sure whether or not he would come. He might have been planning to come, but on another night; she really had no idea. But he came, and he was alone. He came to make sure that it was really true, to see whether Gongorō really was still alive, because that last time they'd all been so sure they had killed him. Tsugumi waited for her chance and then snuck up behind him and bashed him over the head with something. While the guy was still reeling she sealed his mouth with duct tape and pushed him down into the hole. Then she put the board back over the opening, covered it with dirt, and returned to her room.

. . . I had no idea whether this sort of thing was actually even possible. But whether it was or not, Tsugumi had done it. And setting aside the fact that Yōko had stumbled onto the truth, everything had gone just as she'd planned. *I can't understand this. Where does this tenacious energy of hers come from? And the careful precision that gives it shape? And what's its purpose?* What on earth had she been trying to do? I couldn't understand it at all.

I kept thinking about this as I lay in my futon, unable to sleep. It was near dawn now, and when I looked out the window the eastern sky held such a dim hint of light that it seemed I might just be imagining it. After a while I got up and sat staring out toward the dark ocean. But that ocean—the expanse of water that I knew was out there, that had to be out there—was still sunk in the blue depths of the night, so that it seemed to have dropped utterly out of existence, leaving nothing but an enormous void. Gradually this scene worked its way down into the core of my sleepy head.

Tsugumi has just thrown away her life.

Finally this thought—something that Yōko must have understood a good deal earlier—welled up inside me, accompanied by a burst of shock. Kyōichi and the future meant less to her than this—that's how badly she'd wanted to carry this through. Tsugumi had tried to kill a person. At the end of all the work, after struggling through labor so intense it passed well beyond the limits of her body's strength, she seriously believed that the high school kid's death would be a less weighty matter than the death of a dog she had loved.

Again and again I found myself reliving the peculiar excitement I'd sensed in Tsugumi when we'd gotten together earlier in the evening, as she told me about the adventure she'd just had. Tsugumi never changes at all. Her love for Kyōichi, all the months and years she had spent with the rest of us, the new sequence of days that would begin when her family moved away, and Pooch—none of it changed Tsugumi at all, not deep down inside. She hadn't changed a bit ever since she was a child. All along she had been living in a universe of thought that was all her own, shared with no one else.

Every time I thought about all this, an image of Tsugumi sitting with a wide smile on her face, holding the dog that looked just like Gongorō in her arms, flickered across the surface of my mind like a burst of warm sunlight. There wasn't a trace of anything ugly in that scene, and it left me dazzled.

Presence

"My God, use your brain—you think I'd actually try to kill someone?" Tsugumi would sneer. "Hell, I just wanted to put him in kind of a tight spot, you know, give the asshole a little scare, and here you morons are bawling and making a fuss as if it were all real. You two must be the biggest wusses in the world!" And as she jeered, Yōko and I would see that look she always got in her eyes when she was making fun of you.

We had been expecting that.

But Tsugumi was hospitalized immediately. Her temperature zoomed up, her kidneys stopped functioning properly, the over-exertion had left her totally drained of energy . . . as soon as Tsugumi finished her "work," every possible problem erupted into her body, and all at once. She was pounded flat.

Anyone who carried out a job that strenuous would get sick! I thought, as I watched them load her quietly moaning form into the taxi that would take her to the hospital. I just couldn't understand what had made her go so far.

—*Idiot. Didn't it occur to you that I have to go home?*

Her face was bright red and her eyebrows were pinched tightly together; the pain was written on her unconscious face. For some reason seeing her like that made me ache so hard I even hated her for it.

There were still things I wanted to talk about. We were supposed to take Pooch for one last walk, we were going to say goodbye on the beach . . .

Nothing could be done about any of that now, and yet each little regret hit me with a strange pang of sadness. As Aunt Masako climbed into the taxi she muttered, "You're such a fool, Tsugumi." For a moment I couldn't believe what I'd heard, but when my aunt glanced back at me her eyes were smiling softly, as if to say, *What can you do? This is how things are!* She had a change of clothes and a towel for Tsugumi clasped in her arms.

I smiled and waved. The taxi sped off through the autumn sun.

Kyōichi came back the day after Tsugumi was hospitalized.

He said he wanted to talk, so we met that night by the ocean.

"Have you been to see Tsugumi yet?" I asked, since I couldn't think of any other way to begin. The crashing of the waves echoed through the darkness that surrounded us, and as we stood there heavy drops of rain started tumbling down through the strong wind, pounding into us. The lights burning on the boats sailing by in the distance looked blurry.

"Yeah, I saw her. But she looked like she was in a lot of pain, so I couldn't really stay very long. We didn't get to talk much," Kyōichi replied. He had sat down and put his feet up on the breakwater, and now he was staring out across the dark surface of the ocean—I saw his face in profile. His hands remained in his lap, clasped together. They struck me as being unusually big and white. "I take it she was up to something," he continued. "Not that we would have been able to stop her, of course. That girl is such a total master at playing innocent that she makes you feel bad just for being suspicious of her."

I laughed, then told him about the hole. About Yōko's tears.

Kyōichi listened in silence. My voice mingling with the rush of the waves, I painted a perfect picture of Tsugumi. An over-whelmingly clear sense of her presence rose with the wind that streaked through the darkness, fell with the chilly drops of rain that splashed down onto our cheeks. I kept working to change the things she had done into words, and little by little the bril-liant light of Tsugumi's life began to sparkle through the story, flickering up first in one place and then in another, glowing with such ferocious strength that it felt as if she were actually here with us even now. Like the lanterns on the boats that dotted the ocean, revealing its contours, Tsugumi's life shone.

"What a riot. There's no one like her!" chuckled Kyōichi after he'd heard the end of the story, struggling to keep from laugh-ing. "I mean *really*—a hole? What the hell was she thinking?"

"Yeah, you said it." I laughed along with Kyōichi. The night all this stuff happened I'd felt so unnerved and so sorry for Yōko that I hadn't really given the matter any thought, but in retrospect the particular method that Tsugumi had chosen—a technique that managed to be both peculiarly straightforward and somehow oddly twisted—seemed so totally characteristic it was funny.

"You know, sometimes when I'm thinking about Tsugumi . . . well, all of a sudden I'll find myself thinking about these really gigantic things," said Kyōichi. His tone of voice, and the unex-pectedness of his words, made it sound almost like a confession.

"It's not anything I plan, you know—somewhere along the way I just notice that my thoughts have started linking up with all these amazingly big issues. Life, death, stuff like that. And it's not because she's so frail, either. It's just that when I look into her eyes, or when I look at the way she lives her life, for some reason I start feeling sort of solemn."

I knew exactly what he meant. The things he was saying seeped down into the center of my now chilly body, making my chest burn.

Tsugumi's very presence linked us to something huge.

As I stood there in the dark, my feelings strengthened.

"This summer was so much fun," I said. "It's strange, it seems like it only lasted an instant, but it also seems to have lasted an unbelievably long time. I'm glad you were here with us. I'm sure Tsugumi's never had such a good time."

"She'll be all right, I feel sure she will," said Kyōichi.

I nodded firmly in agreement. It felt as if the loud roaring of the wind and the waves was turning the ground at our feet into something ambiguous. I gazed up for a long time at the scattering of bright stars that filled the sky, as if I were trying to count them. "After all, she's been hospitalized lots of times before," I said. But my voice was lost in the dark.

Kyōichi was staring out over the sea. He had a look in his eyes so fragile it seemed as if the wind might whittle it away into nothing. He looked sadder and more lonely than ever before.

Tsugumi will no longer be a part of this town. Their young love will have to move into a new configuration . . . all those things that can't really be put into words must be churning now in Kyōichi's heart. Just a short while ago, so recently it almost seems as if you could reach out and touch it all, we used to see the two of them and the two dogs walking

*on this same beach—don't forget that. Days spent mingling with the
landscape of this shore, a perfectly ordinary part of the beach . . . those
days were blessed.*

That night remains in my heart as a truly wonderful scene.

For a long time after that, so long that our hair ended up
drenched, the two of us stood there together without exchang-
ing a word. We gazed out vaguely toward the farthest reaches
of the ocean, in perfect understanding.

I went to visit Tsugumi the day before my return to Tokyo.

In order to avoid being embarrassed by Tsugumi's foul behavior, my aunt had arranged for her to be given a room of her
own. There was no response when I knocked, so I opened the
door without saying anything.

Tsugumi was asleep.

Her white skin still had the same smooth sheen as always, but
she looked terribly emaciated. The long eyelashes on her closed
lids and the hair that fanned across her pillow and everything
else about her looked so pristine and lovely that you could almost believe she was a real-life Sleeping Beauty, and it scared
me to look at her. I felt as if the Tsugumi I knew had vanished.

"Hey, wake up!" I said, patting Tsugumi's cheek.

She moaned and opened her eyes. Her jewellike pupils stared
back at me, very large in her small face. "Ah-h-h-h-h, why'd you
have to wake me?" she whimpered in a very nasal voice, and then
rubbed her eyes.

I smiled at her, relieved. "I came to say goodbye. I'm heading home, you know," I said. "But I want you to hurry up and
get better, okay?"

"You're what! I can't believe you're so cruel!" Tsugumi said. Her voice sounded dreadful, as if it had taken all she had just to pronounce those words. Evidently she didn't have the energy to sit up, because she just kept glaring at me from where she was, flat on her back.

"It's your own fault. You get what you deserve." I grinned.

"Yeah, I guess that's true." Tsugumi smiled faintly. And then she said it: "Listen to me, kid. I'm not going to tell anyone else about this, but I've got a feeling this is the end. I'm dying."

My body stiffened. I sat down hurriedly in the chair by her bed, right beside her. "What on earth are you talking about?" I said. I felt somewhat bewildered, somewhat disbelieving. "I mean, they say you're getting better every day, right? Everything's progressing just as it should, isn't it? Are you trying to say there's something else wrong this time? You know, a big part of the reason your parents are keeping you in the hospital like this is to keep you from doing anything too wild while you're getting better. They're using this like a mental hospital or something. This isn't a matter of life or death at all. Seriously, get a grip on yourself."

"No, this time it's different," Tsugumi said, her expression deadly serious. The shadow I saw in her eyes now was more dark and earnest than anything I had ever seen in her before. "You get what I'm saying, right? Whether you live or die, you know— it has nothing to do with the kind of crap you're talking about. Maria, I don't feel like going on anymore. I really don't."

"Tsugumi?" I said.

"Trust me, nothing like this has ever happened before," Tsugumi went on, her voice faltering. "It didn't matter how bad things got, it didn't matter what was happening, until now I've

never felt such a total lack of interest in things. Right now I don't
care about anything. I'm serious, it really feels like some part of
me is gone. In the past I didn't give a damn about death, you
know, but now it terrifies me. Even when I try to stir myself
up, I just get irritated because I can't make anything come out.
And in the middle of the night I lie here thinking about all this.
If I don't get back on track somehow, I'm dead, that's the sense
I get. There isn't a single strong emotion inside me. That's a first
for me, Maria. I mean, I don't even hate anything. It's like I've
turned into a boring twit of a cliché, just another damn wispy
bedridden girl. I can understand how that babe in the O. Henry
story felt as she watched the leaves fall off that vine one by one,
how honestly frightened it must have made her. I think about
how the people around me will start treating me like some kind
of incompetent ass as I get ever weaker and weaker, even compared to the way I was before, how they'll be making fun of me,
and about how I'll slowly start to fade away, and it just makes
me feel like I'm losing my mind."

"But . . ." I fell silent. It stunned me to realize that she really
seemed to mean what she was saying. But what was most sur-
prising was that she seemed never to have felt these things before—the arrogance of it was astonishing. Had she been scared
to think that things might not work out with Kyōichi after her
family moved? Or had the things Yōko said hit her too hard?
Because it was true—just as Tsugumi had said, the energy her
entire body had always radiated, no matter how sick and weak
she got, was starting to vanish. I could sense that. "Listen," I said.
"If you can make a speech like that, you're fine."

Tsugumi was staring out uneasily at the sky.

"It'd be nice if that were true."

She turned to look at me. I had peered into these eyes thousands, tens of thousands of times since the two of us were small, eyes as clear as glass beads—there was no trace of a lie in them now. *A profound sparkle that never changes, a sparkle that seems to sing of the glory of eternity.*

"Of course it's true," I replied.

But to tell the truth, the idea that, for the first time in her life, Tsugumi was suffering the same torments as the rest of the world really did scare me. *If she loses her spunkiness, maybe she really will die,* I thought. But I couldn't let her know . . .

"Well, I'm going." I stood up.

"WHAT!" she cried. "I can't believe you!"

This time her voice was pretty loud.

I wanted to keep our goodbyes nice and dry, make them as quick and casual as a little boy's when he saunters out of the room. I jerked open the door, glancing back only as I walked out.

"See you later."

And then I turned my back on her. *You asshole! You're such a jerk! Is this actually happening? We might never see each other again, and you're telling me school is more important! Oh my GOD! What a monster! You realize that's why you're so unpopular, yeah? Man, you . . .* The background music of Tsugumi's furious cursing kept flowing on behind me as I sauntered down the hall of the hospital.

It was night when I stepped outside.

I sensed a faint breath of salt in the cool breeze—it was as if the ocean that surrounded the peninsula had enveloped every nook and cranny of the town. Walking along the darkened street, I felt a little bit of an urge to cry.

* * *

The next day the sky was as clear as it could be, and a hot sun burned down with such blinding strength it was like the middle of summer. Even so, the incredible clarity of the rays made you feel the autumn.

I felt a tug of pain during breakfast. It was almost as if the whole table and all the fresh seafood that Aunt Masako always went to buy at the market every morning and the general atmosphere created by the meals she prepared and all the rest was being slowly burned into my heart. I ate cheerily, boisterously.

"Tsugumi really is hopeless, isn't she? Now she won't even be able to see you off." Aunt Masako laughed. She'd spoken in exactly the same buoyant tone she used to ask Yōko if she wanted any more to eat. And so as I sat there flooded in morning sunlight, I found myself believing once again what I had already confirmed for myself any number of times—that Tsugumi really was going to be all right. Aunt Masako was packing some pickled vegetables and a mixture of boiled foods into two plastic containers. She wrapped the boxes in a white cloth and started tying a tight knot at the top. "Give these to your mom as a present from me, okay?" she said. Watching her fingers flit deftly about as she did all this, I could already feel myself starting to miss her.

When the time came for me to go, my aunt and uncle came and saw me off at the front door, standing on the stoop. Yōko said she would go with me to the bus stop and went off to get her bicycle. I said goodbye to Pooch.

Then I turned to my aunt and uncle. "Thanks for everything."

"Come and see us at the pension," replied my uncle, smiling.

"It was a nice summer, wasn't it?" said my aunt.

Leaving the Yamamoto Inn behind me for good, walking away through the burning rays of the sun, really wasn't hard at all. I just stepped out the door the way I did every time I went to buy a soda, and by the time I turned to look back I was already far away. I got a glimpse of my aunt's and uncle's backs as the two of them went into the inn.

Yōko and I started walking again, side by side.

She kept squinting into the bright sunlight, the rays hitting us straight on, and as she strode on next to me the fact of her shortness and the way her hair swished across her shoulders with every step she took sank deep into my heart, as if it had all been specially pieced together for a scene in some movie. The row of old inns that lined the narrow street leading to the bus stop. The withered shades of the bindweed flowers that had been planted everywhere, all along the street. My memories will remain here, closed within this dry noon. Encased within the unique feeling of noon in a town by the ocean.

We sat down on the concrete steps of the ticket office at the bus stop, and each of us ate a Popsicle.

I doubt it would even be possible to count up the number of Popsicles Yōko and I have eaten together over the summers. As far back as it was possible for either of us to remember, we had been going out together to buy Popsicles with our allowance money. Tsugumi would steal Yōko's and cram them into her mouth, a whole Popsicle in one bite, showing no mercy, making Yōko cry.

A surge of emotion cuts into my chest, overwhelmingly fierce. As if these people I love and this town are going to vanish from the very face of the earth, a feeling so overwhelmingly bright I can't stand to look at it straight on.

Shielding her eyes with her hand, Yōko looked up at the sky. "I wonder if these will be our last Popsicles of the year," she said.

"Nah," I grinned. "We'll find an excuse to eat more."

"For some reason I just feel so bummed out, you know?" murmured Yōko. "Just think, next month we'll be moving . . . I don't know, somehow it just doesn't feel true to me, I don't quite get it. I don't think any of this will really hit me until the time comes when we actually have to leave."

Yōko looked at me and smiled. She seemed very calm. You got the sense that she'd made up her mind not to let herself cry today.

"Cousins are cousins as long as they live," I said. "It doesn't matter where in the world they are."

"Yup. And sisters are sisters as long as they live." Yōko giggled.

"Tsugumi's been kind of weird lately, hasn't she?" I said. "Do you think maybe it's because she doesn't want to move? Or did she put so much energy into digging that hole and all that she just burned herself out? I'm not sure what to make of her now." Half of me wondered whether Yōko was feeling the same unease.

"Hmmm . . . I'm not . . . I don't think that's it. You're right that she's different from usual, I know what you mean. It's like her thoughts have gotten stuck somewhere, you know, something like that. She acts the same as always with Kyōichi, but then . . . well, I go to see her, right? But she doesn't even answer when I knock on the door. So I just open the door and walk in, not calling in or anything because I don't want to wake her up if she's sleeping, and she looks really surprised and hides something in her bed—it looks like it must be some sort of paper. I ask her what she thinks she's doing, tell her she has to get some rest instead of fooling around, and then when I leave the room to get some hot water for tea or something—you know how you keep stepping out for a moment to do stuff like that—well, I go off and get whatever it is and then come back, right, and she's working at it again, writing something."

"Writing?" I asked, surprised.

"Yeah, she seems to be writing something. And you know, if she's going to throw herself that deeply into whatever it is she's doing, she's simply never going to get well. Even if her chances of recovering are good, it's too much . . . I really wonder what that girl is thinking."

"She still has a fever, right?"

"Yes. It zooms way up at night and then goes down again every morning, just the same thing over and over."

"What do you think she's writing? A poem or a story or something?" I cocked my head, puzzled. Tsugumi and the act of "writing" struck me as such an unlikely pair that I hardly knew what to think.

Yōko grinned at me. "I never understand what's going on in Tsugumi's mind."

I don't think I'll ever forget her elegant manner, the soft feeling of dignity that tinted all the kind, helpful things she did. Just like Tsugumi, she would continue to live and grow as a pale shadow in the recesses of my heart. From now on, no matter where I was, whatever sort of person I grew up to be.

"It sure is hot today, isn't it? It feels like the middle of summer." Yōko looked up at the sky again as she spoke, and I gazed at the round silhouette of her chin. Yes, it was strange. I was seeing everything so clearly. Almost as if I were viewing it all through a special wide-angle lens, taking in a full 180 degrees. I sat there, sunk in a very quiet mood, breathing in all that there was in this town, the town where I had grown up.

The bus pulled slowly in.

I couldn't shake off the vague feeling of sadness that clung to me as I stood in the brightness of noon, not even when it was time to board the bus.

—*If only Tsugumi had been here, if only she'd been able to come and make all this vanish with that powerful light of hers. If only she had come to sneer at us, make fun of the lonely expressions on our faces.*

Looking out at Yōko through the window of the bus as she kept waving her hand, hardly moving it, still waving as she fell away into the distance, I knew that all I'd really wanted was Tsugumi's presence there with us.

It was raining in Tokyo.

I don't know if it was because the weather was different, or because of the chill in the air, or because it was so crowded, but when I stepped out onto the platform of the train station near our apartment, everything had an oddly unanchored look to it, as if it were all hovering in the air.

I suppose it was just my state of mind.

I'd come back, this was my homecoming, and yet everything seemed so far away it was like a scene I'd encountered once in a dream. My body brimmed with energy from the month I'd spent sucking in lungfuls of sea breeze, going around the town, simply moving around.

Walking through the gate, staring out into the gray of the rain-misty city, my thoughts turned for no real reason in an unexpected direction.

My real life is just beginning.

I wobbled down the crowded stairs, struggling with my giant

bag, and found my mother standing at the bottom. Surprised, I hurried over.

"Mom! What are you doing here?"

She was holding the basket she used when she went shopping. She smiled. "I was out shopping anyway, so I thought I'd come meet you. You don't have an umbrella, do you?"

"Nope."

"Well, we can go home together."

My mother and I started walking side by side. I could feel my mother's presence pushing me back toward reality, one step at a time.

"Did you have a nice time?"

"You bet."

"That sure is some tan, Maria."

"Yeah, it was sunny out every day."

"And I hear Tsugumi has a boyfriend! Your father was surprised."

"Yeah. They spent all summer together and got really close."

"And Tsugumi is back in the hospital? She'd been doing so well."

"I have a feeling this summer was too much for her."

We walked on through the rain, sharing a single umbrella. My mother's voice was very quiet. We were heading down a street lined on both sides with stores, toward our apartment, and deep inside I was beginning to realize with even greater clarity just how hot the summer had been. And at the same time I was thinking more tenderly of Tsugumi than ever before.

Tsugumi in love. That brilliant face.

"Your father has been waiting. He was so eager to get you back it wouldn't surprise me if he came home early today. To

tell the truth, it was a bit boring for me too while you were away.
I'm planning to make all your favorite foods tonight, you know.
How does that sound?"

My mother smiled.

"Boy, it'll really be nice to eat at home. It's been so long since
I last tasted your cooking. And we have so much to talk about,"
I said.

But even as I said this, I was thinking that I probably wouldn't
tell them about the hole. Or about how deep Kyōichi's love for
Tsugumi was when he stood near the dark ocean, or about the
awful weight of Yōko's tears. Because these things could never
be communicated, these treasures of my heart.

And so my summer came to an end.

A Letter from Tsugumi

I felt kind of lost for a while after I went back to Tokyo.

Of course school was packed with people like that, still muddle-headed from the effects of summer vacation. In the beginning my classmates and I all kept making the same observation, saying that it felt as if we were actually just little kids playing school, pretending. And yet each time I had a conversation with someone about what we'd done during the break, I couldn't help feeling that the summer I'd passed had been a little different from everyone else's.

Yes, I really had been in a different world.

The ferocious energy Tsugumi gave off, the strong sunlight on the summer beach, the new friend I'd made . . . it had all blended together to create a space unlike any I'd ever been in. A world sturdier and more powerful than reality, as vivid as the dreams soldiers have just before they die, when they see the towns they were born in. And yet here in this weak September light I found myself empty-handed, without even a trace of the summer left in me, not an inkling of its past presence. All I could say when people asked me what I had done was that I'd spent the whole time back in the town where I'd grown up, staying for free at an inn run by some relatives. For me the summer had been the concentrated essence of everything in the past that I loved and missed.

And every time I thought about this, I'd wonder.

Had Tsugumi felt the same way?

One day my father broke his leg.

Apparently he'd been climbing a ladder in his company's storeroom when he tumbled off and plunged to the floor, still clasping a big load of materials that he'd taken from one of the highest shelves. My mother and I sped to the hospital in a chaos of agitation and found my father in bed, smiling sheepishly. Emotional pain really gets to him, but he can handle physical pain.

My mother and I went back home, both feeling very relieved, and then my mother headed out to the hospital again to take my father the clothes he would need for his two or three days of hospitalization. I was left at home all alone.

It was then that the phone rang.

Something told me this was a phone call I wasn't going to like. The first thing that drifted into my mind when I heard the ring was an image of my father's face. So I lifted the receiver very slowly.

"Hello?"

But it was Yōko.

"Are your mom and dad around?"

"Nope. As a matter of fact my dad broke his leg, and he's in the hospital. He must be the biggest bozo around." I laughed.

But Yōko didn't join me in laughing.

And then she said it. "Something's wrong with Tsugumi."

I fell silent. I was remembering Tsugumi's white profile, the way it had been when I went to visit her, how she had insisted that she was going to die. Come to think of it, these instincts of hers never missed the mark.

"What do you mean?" I finally managed to say. "What's wrong?"

"Until noon today the doctors were saying that she'd probably pull through all right, but she's hardly been conscious at all since yesterday, and she has this terrible fever . . . All of a sudden things seem to have gotten worse."

"Is she allowed to have visitors?"

"No, not right now. But my mom and I are staying in the hospital."

Yōko's voice was very calm. I could sense how difficult she was finding it even now to accept that all this was really happening.

"Okay, I'll come down first thing tomorrow morning," I said. "No matter what her condition is like, we'll take turns watching over her, okay?" My voice sounded as calm as Yōko's, precisely the opposite of how I felt inside. It echoed with the force of a pledge. "Have you told Kyōichi?"

"Yeah, I called him. He said he'd be right over."

"Yōko—" I said, "if anything should happen, you know, I want you to give me a call right away, even if it's the middle of the night."

"Sure, of course."

The call was over.

I told my mother the bad news when she got back home, and she suggested that we leave my father to his own devices the next day and go down to help take care of Tsugumi. We set about preparing for the trip.

I pulled the phone into my room and set it close to my pillow before I went to bed. *What if it rings . . . ?* In the depth of the night, my sleep was shallow. And all during that ambiguous sleep, within the coming and going fragments of dreams, I continued to feel the existence of that phone. All night it was there, a sensation as cold and unpleasant as a rusty mass of iron.

Yōko and Tsugumi were never absent from my dreams. The scenes were infuriatingly disconnected, and each time I got a glimpse of Tsugumi through that fury I would slip into a mood that was sacred, slightly sweet. The look on her face was as surly as usual, and she would be out on the beach or back at the Yamamoto Inn, making various apparently impudent comments, just the way she always had. And yet as ordinary as it all was, I felt uneasy being with her. Being with Tsugumi, just like always.

The morning sunlight came streaming straight down over my shut eyelids, and I groaned and sat up. The phone hadn't rung. Wondering how things were going with Tsugumi, I opened the curtains.

It was a lovely morning.

Autumn was definitely here. The sky echoed with the clear tones of a pale faintly greenish blue, the blue stretching on and on as far as your eye could see, and the trees swayed slowly back and forth, cutting wide arcs into the sweeping autumn wind.

Everything was steeped in the tranquil fragrance of autumn, and it all came together to form a soundless and translucent world. It felt as if it had been ages since I'd tasted the joy of a morning this dazzlingly bright, and for a while I just sat there with a blank mind, gazing out at the land before me. It was all projected so clearly into my head that it made my heart ache.

We had no idea how Tsugumi was doing now, but my mother and I made up our minds that either way we should go and see. We were eating breakfast in preparation for starting out when the telephone rang.

It was Aunt Masako.

"How is she?" I asked.

And my aunt began, "Well, to tell the truth . . ." There was a slight twinge of embarrassment in her voice. She laughed.

"You mean she's okay?" I asked.

"Yes, she's okay," said my aunt. "To tell the truth, she's made a complete turnaround and is doing so well now that it's as if nothing was ever wrong to begin with. I guess maybe we went a little overboard."

"Are you serious?"

I felt all the tension draining from my body.

"Late yesterday afternoon her condition suddenly took a turn for the worse, you see, and since that sort of thing hadn't happened for quite a while we may have jumped to conclusions a bit too quickly. The doctors decided that things were looking bad, and they did absolutely everything they could, they were just wonderful . . . and they were all amazed at how strong Tsugumi is, you know, her will to live. For a while I really thought we might be headed for something awful, but this morning she's just as settled as she could be, as if yesterday were all a lie, and she's in there sleeping like a baby . . . We've been through all sorts of agony because of Tsugumi's health, but this is the first time I've ever had to deal with anything like this. Of course, you can be sure lots more unexpected things will happen in the future, but . . ." Aunt Masako said this with resignation, but her tone was bright. "Anyway, I'm sorry we gave you such a scare. If something really does happen we'll give you a call right away and make you come give us a hand, so don't worry about coming today. Just stay put and take it easy. Sorry again for making you anxious."

"Well, I'm glad to hear she's all right," I said. Together with the feeling of relief that hit me, I felt a stream of something warm surging up into my heart, as if my blood had just started circulating again. I lobbed the phone over to my mother and went back to my room, then snuggled down into my bed. Washed in morning sun, I closed my eyes and went to sleep listening to the distant murmur of my mother's delighted voice. This time I was able to fall asleep right away, and I was very solidly out.

It was a deep, gentle sleep.

A few days later, exactly at noon, I got a call from Tsugumi.

"Howdy, ugly wretch!" I'd hardly finished lifting the receiver and saying hello when her voice came hurtling out of the phone, and all at once, in some space beyond thought, the knowledge crashed over me that it would have been absolutely unthinkable for me to lose this voice. Never to hear the familiar, faltering, past-recalling, high-pitched quiver of Tsugumi's voice. I could hear a clamor of voices on the other end of the line, names being called out over a microphone, the screams of children crying.

"What's up with you? Are you still at the hospital?" I asked. "Are you feeling okay now? You aren't sick anymore?"

"Yeah, I'm fine. And yes, I'm in the hospital," Tsugumi replied, and then started saying things that made no sense. "Kinda sounds like it hasn't gotten there yet, though, doesn't it? Very odd. I can't believe stuff like this actually happens. That dumb pinhead of a nurse must have heard the address wrong. She must be the biggest ass in the world."

"Tsugumi? What are you talking about?" I asked, wondering if maybe the fever had done something to her mind. But she made no response, provided no answer to my question. The silence lasted so long that I found myself calling an image of her into my mind. A single composite Tsugumi, pieced together from all the different situations I had ever seen her in . . . Her fine, flowing hair, the fiery light in her eyes, her thin wrists. The lines of her ankles when she walks barefoot, her perfectly white teeth when she smiles. The tilt of her eyebrows as she scowls, her face turned to the side, and the ocean she's looking at. The shore swept by shining waves . . .

"See, I was dying," Tsugumi said suddenly, very clearly.

"Oh give me a break!" I said, laughing. "You come trotting down the hall of the hospital just as healthy as can be, and then come out with this dying stuff? You ought to know better than that, Tsugumi."

"God, you're such an idiot! I almost died, really! My sense of everything slipped way off into the distance, and I saw this enormous light, and I felt this urge to go toward it, you know . . . but then as I drew closer, my dear departed mother appeared and called out, *No, no, you mustn't come here! . . .*"

"Lies from start to finish. Just which mother of yours has died?"

Tsugumi hadn't been this lively in a while, and I was glad she was.

"True, that was a lie. But I mean it, things really did get pretty dangerous. I just kept getting weaker and weaker every day, you know, and I seriously felt that this time I couldn't make it," Tsugumi said. "So I wrote you a letter."

"A letter?" I blurted out, startled. "To me?"

"That's right," Tsugumi said. "It's pretty damn hard to believe I could be such a wuss, but there you go. And here I am, still alive. Of course moaning about it doesn't change a thing. The nurse I asked to take care of the damned letter says she's already sent it, so there you go, I couldn't get it back if I tried. I'd tell you to throw it away without opening it, but you're such a nasty little weasel that you'd read it anyway. So what the hell, go ahead and read it."

"Which is it, Tsugumi? Should I read it or not?"

Tsugumi has written me a letter . . .

The thought was strangely exciting.

"I don't care. Go ahead and read it," Tsugumi said, a laugh in her voice. "After what I've just been through, I do sort of feel like I've died and come back. So maybe what I said in that letter was true. I get the feeling that from now on I may start changing, little by little."

I didn't quite understand what Tsugumi was trying to say. And yet I had the feeling that somewhere down inside I did understand, and for a moment I found it impossible to reply. Then Tsugumi spoke.

"Listen, Kyōichi just walked over, so I'll put him on. Ciao."

I tried to call her back, but apparently she was already gone. At first all I heard was Kyōichi shouting, "Go on, get back to your room!" Then he picked up the receiver and said hello, without having any idea at all who he was talking to.

You just can't get any more egocentric than Tsugumi. She was probably already striding down the hall toward her room. Her small body, sticking her chest out with all the pompous self-assuredness of a king.

I smiled wryly and returned his hello.

"Oh Maria, it's you, huh?" Kyōichi laughed.

"I hear things were pretty bad with Tsugumi," I said.

"Yeah, but she sure seems to be in awfully good shape now," Kyōichi said. "I don't get it at all. I mean, for a time they weren't even letting her have visitors or anything, you know, that's how bad things got. It sure gave me a fright, let me tell you."

"Well, give her my best, will you? We didn't get to talk much," I said. And then, very smoothly, the question slipped from my mouth. "Kyōichi? Tell me, do you think that when Tsugumi goes off to live in their new pension in the mountains the two of you will just naturally drift apart?"

"Hmm. I don't think I can really say what the future will bring until I've actually seen what it's like being apart, but I find it hard to believe that I'll come across many girls as intense as Tsugumi. She's such a great kid, she really is, you just can't beat her. I'm sure I'll never forget this summer. And even if we do break up, she's been carved so intensely into my mind and my heart that the mark she's left will stay in me my whole life. I can tell you that for sure," Kyōichi said, speaking very calmly. "And don't forget that from now on our hotel will be here for you all, even if the Yamamoto Inn isn't. You can all come and stay whenever you like."

"So I guess we'll still be connected somehow or other even after this, right? Just like we were this summer?"

"I bet you're right." Kyōichi chuckled. "Hold on—Yōko just walked into the lobby. Wow, she's got a bunch of lilies with her and, oh, oh . . . oh man! She just smashed into a patient at the corner of one of the halls, and now she's apologizing to the person . . . all right, yeah, here she comes, here she comes! Okay, I'll pass you over to her. Bye."

Yōko came on the line, saying, *Hello? Who on earth am I talking to?* and I answered. It occurred to me that it was like a parade—they just keep coming. I sat down on the chair next to our phone and kept chatting with Yōko, gazing up at the sky outside. The noon sun poured down, lighting up the room and its squareness. And I felt a quiet sense of determination rising up into me, slowly flooding me, but without assuming any particular shape, and, of course, for no reason I could understand. *From now on this is where I will live.*

Dear Maria,

Well, things have turned out just as I said they would.

In fact you may be on your way here to attend my funeral when this letter arrives. This is the real "Haunted Mailbox."

Having a funeral in autumn is so lonely, no fun at all.

Over the past few days I've written you a hell of a lot of letters. I'd write one and then tear it up and then start writing again. I don't know why it has to be you, of all people. But for some reason I can't help thinking that of all the people around me, only you can really read the meanings of the words I use, and understand what I'm saying.

And so, now that death really does seem to be bearing down on me, this notion of leaving a letter behind for you has become my only hope, the one wish left in this heart of mine. When I imagine all the rest of them standing around crying until it no longer even has any meaning, coming up with their own pleasant interpretations of who I was—let me tell you, it makes me want to puke. Kyōichi is worth keeping an eye on, I'll give you that, but love is a battle, and you can't ever let your lover see your weaknesses, not even when you arrive at the very end.

Why is it that as much of an airhead as you are, you still manage to take stock of things, to look at the world in such a bighearted, reliable way? I just don't get it at all.

One other thing. Right after I came to the hospital this time, I read a novel called The Dead Zone. I only started reading it to help make the time pass, but it was much more engaging than I'd expected, and I ended up reading it straight through. I started feeling worse and worse, my breath was coming in gasps—but for someone whose body is as fragile as mine, *watching the main character keep growing steadily weaker and weaker was a pretty heartrending experience. The main character gets smashed up in a car accident, and it's about what happens after that, one thing piled on top of another, all these horrible things that keep pushing him on toward death, and the final chapter has these letters addressed to his father and his father's girlfriend that he leaves behind when he dies. They're letters from the dead zone. And you know, when I read that part even I couldn't help shedding a few tears. And I found myself feeling extremely envious of the guy, really yearning to be able to try this business of writing a letter and having someone receive it. That's why I'm writing this now.*

Those days when I was digging away at my hole, hoping to drop that wretched little brat down into it, I kept thinking about all sorts of things. To pass the time while I worked, you know— on-the-job entertainment. And then, the night everything happened, as I listened to all that stuff Yōko said through her tears, knowing that the big idiot might very well go on looking after me just as she always has, never even going off to get married—listening to her then, I began to understand things even better than I had outside, in an even more violent rush. I felt as if I had gotten a clear look at the boundaries of who I am. I saw myself as nothing but this pale little girl surrounded by people barely able to keep her flimsy body from collapsing, a girl who has lived her life from one day to the next thinking only of herself, running around throwing tantrums, and I realized that I would probably be like this for the rest of my life.

Of course it's not like I'm having second thoughts about the way I've lived or anything, and I've known about all of this for a long time.

It's just that it felt strangely good to let these thoughts drift through my mind while I was in that state, working at the outer limit of what my body could take, feeling as if I might faint—and soon I found myself unable to shake the feeling that I would be dying within just a few days. After all, it seems reasonable to say that digging a hole as deep as the one I made would be a pretty major undertaking even for someone in good health. I found it a painful task, very well suited to be the last of my life.

And since I was digging that hole in the neighbors' garden, not ours, there was no way I could let anyone find out. I only worked at night. Dragging the soil out and away little by little, I continued to dig.

Toward the end the hole really got deep, and when I looked up from the bottom I could see the stars. The earth was hard, and my hands got cuts all over them, and every day I would stare into the coming summer dawn.

From the bottom of my hole.

Through the small circle of vision open to me I would watch as the sky grew slowly lighter and the stars faded away, and in my exhaustion I would think about a whole lot of different things. I wore a bathing suit and on top of that the same muddy jacket every day so that there would be no muddy clothes to tip off my mother. And I noticed that I had hardly any memories of ever putting on my bathing suit and going to swim in the ocean. In swimming class I would just sit and watch, memorizing the strokes—when I actually thought about it, I realized that I don't even know how to do the crawl. And I remembered how every day I would run out of breath at the same spot on that hill we climbed on the way to school, and how I had never once participated in the morning assembly, when everyone had to stand for such a long time. Back when all that was happening, I never paid any attention to the trivial things that were happening right in front of me, I just kept gazing up at the blue sky overhead. I didn't notice those things.

It aches when I breathe, and my body feels so heavy it's as if the cover has me pinned down, keeping me from moving.

I can't even get down a decent meal. About the only things I can eat are the pickled vegetables the old hag brings, and stuff like that. My God, Maria, doesn't that make you laugh? Doesn't it?

Until now it didn't matter how bad things got, somewhere way down inside I always had this place that was totally fine, just as strong and healthy as it could be. But now the warehouse is empty. I'm really hurting now. I feel so bad I'm finally going to give in and tell the truth.

I can't stand the nights.

When they put out the lights here this room turns into an enormous universe of dark, and I start feeling so low I don't know what to do. It's so terrible that I almost start to cry. But crying wears me down. So I lie here in the darkness, struggling to hold it in. I write this letter by the beam of a small flashlight. My awareness of things drifts off into the distance and then returns— my head is whirling. If anything in me snags it'll be like falling off a log. I'll be a miserable little corpse, and all you idiots will run around crying your eyes out.

Every morning an ugly nurse comes and opens my curtains.

Waking up is the pits. My mouth is parched, my head is heavy with pain—the fever has dried me up so completely that I feel like a mummy. And if anything isn't up to scratch, they don't hesitate to start giving me intravenous fluids and all the rest. Believe me, it's the pits.

But when the nurse throws back the curtains and opens the window, the sea breeze comes blowing in with the sunlight. I lie with my eyes still half closed, slipping sleepily through the brightness of my eyelids into a dream about walking the dog.

Because my life was bullshit. If you ask me to say something nice about it, that's about all I can think up. That's what it was worth.

Whatever, I'm glad I'll be able to die in this town.

Keep well.

Tsugumi